PM Teachers' Guide

Emerald Level

Lesley Wing Jan

NELSON
THOMSON LEARNING

Australia · Canada · Mexico · Singapore · Spain · United Kingdom · United States

The PM Library is published by Nelson Thomson Learning and is distributed as follows:

AUSTRALIA
Nelson Thomson Learning
102 Dodds Street
South Melbourne 3205
Victoria

NEW ZEALAND
Nelson Price Milburn
1 Te Puni Street
Petone
Wellington

UNITED KINGDOM
Nelson Thornes
Delta Place
27 Bath Road
Cheltenham GL53 7TH

First published in 2001
10 9 8 7 6 5 4 3 2 1
05 04 03 02 01

PM Teachers' Guide: Emerald Level
ISBN 1 86961 449 6

Written by Lesley Wing Jan
Computer Task Centre Activity Cards by Lynn Davie
Edited by Anna Fern and Kate McGough
Text designed by Heather Jones
Cover designed by Sonia Juraja
Illustrations by Boris Silvestri
Printed in Australia by McPherson's Print Group

Nelson Australia Pty Limited ACN 058 280 149 (incorporated in Victoria) trading as Nelson Thomson Learning.

Contents

About the PM books at Emerald Level

The PM books at Emerald Level comprise:

- twelve fiction chapter books
- an anthology of fiction, non-fiction and verse
- six non-fiction books

The PM books at Emerald Level have been developed to provide a range of titles for students who have become successful readers using the PM titles at lower levels, and who are fluent in their reading. Each title has been written, edited, illustrated and carefully levelled so that students can continue to enjoy reading success while being introduced to new characters and concepts, new ways of presenting text and a range of new genres.

The Emerald Level texts will involve children in reading experiences that build on and extend their reading skills and knowledge, and develop their understanding of both the real and imagined world.

The books provide contexts for the development of reading skills, the exploration of content, themes and ideas in texts, as well as the study of the structure and language used in a range of text types.

Using the books in this range will encourage children to read for different purposes, and help them to understand the need for responsive reading that may involve listening, talking, thinking, doing and other activities from which they can learn further from the reading experience.

The suggested approach to the reading of these books is based on small group teaching and reading (often referred to as guided reading). This approach is based on the premise that

there need to be opportunities for less experienced readers to develop their literacy skills with the support of a more experienced language user. Students need opportunities to learn and talk about the act of reading, the text, its organisation, language features and its social and cultural context. Students need to develop as critical readers who think about and question what they are reading. The small group situations enable this to happen in a supportive environment.

Instructional texts, such as those provided at PM Emerald Level, facilitate this development because they have been written with a variety of purposes in mind:

- enjoyment;
- ease of reading;
- acquisition of knowledge about known and unknown topics;
- provision of a broad range of vocabulary for close study;
- provision of material for discussion of contemporary ideas within a group;
- familiarising students with a variety of text types;
- providing a range of material of different lengths, but of similar difficulty level for contrast and comparison.

Chapter books

The twelve chapter books provide a selection of stories chosen for their broad range of content, characters, topics for discussion, narrative and points of view. They were specifically written with the needs of small group teaching in mind. Topics (which include shoplifting, pool safety, resourcefulness in an emergency, personal responsibility, asthma, wearing a hearing aid, the sadness of separation, and telling fibs) give plenty of scope for group discussion.

The books are grouped into two sets. Set A is for Level 25 and Set B for Level 26. On the inside back cover of each book is a list of the titles in that set in order of difficulty. A synopsis for each title, plus detailed teaching notes, appear on pp.26–49. Related blackline masters appear on pp.70–93. Computer-related task centre activity cards for each title appear on pp.112–123.

Non-fiction: technology in action

The non-fiction titles have a student-centred technology focus, linked broadly to technology outcomes in state and national curriculum documents. They include a range of text types: journal, information narrative, procedure, verse, report, recount, diary, newspaper report, discussion through persuasive letters. Each book has a contents page, a glossary, a list of related websites, and an index. A synopsis of each title plus detailed teaching notes appear on pp.50–61. Accompanying blackline masters appear on pp.94–105. Computer-related task centre activity cards for each title appear on pp.124–129.

Anthology

The anthology contains a selection of fiction, non-fiction and verse. It provides a range of material of similar difficulty levels, yet of completely different lengths, from short verse to fiction extracts of between 300 and 900 words and non-fiction pieces of around 550 words. The longest piece is a chapter-book-length story of 1294 words. Texts within the anthology can be used together for comparison and contrast. All are gently humorous, and the extracts from longer novels provide tastes of literature from well-known writers, which may encourage children to read the complete book. A synopsis of each extract plus detailed teaching notes appear on pp.62–68. Accompanying blackline masters appear on pp.106–107. A computer-related task centre activity card appears on p.130. The study of various texts within the anthology provides opportunities for:

- theme studies in which several texts on the same theme are examined to identify how each writer has dealt with a common theme;
- author studies in which one author's work is examined or analysed, or work by different authors is compared and contrasted;
- genre studies in which similar text types are used to identify common features.

General outcomes

Through the reading of, discussions about and activities associated with each book, the children will have opportunities to do the following:

- develop a positive attitude toward reading and books;
- read and interpret a range of text types;
- read for a range of purposes;
- identify the ways texts are structured and language is used for different purposes and audiences;
- identify the ways writers use language to convey meaning;
- use a variety of strategies for reading for different purposes;
- explore the range and level of responses to reading;
- discuss and justify their own opinions and interpretations of what they have read;
- develop higher-level comprehension and thinking skills.

Small group teaching and reading

Small group teaching and reading provides opportunities for children with similar reading abilities and development to interact, under the guidance of the teacher, with a text that is selected to meet their reading needs. Each child has an individual copy of the text and, with the support of the teacher, is assisted to develop and identify a range of reading strategies, knowledge and responses.

The role of the teacher during small group teaching and reading is to:

- prepare the children for the reading of the book, or parts thereof;
- demonstrate what experienced readers do;
- monitor the children's reading and assist them to identify and develop appropriate reading strategies and knowledge;
- provide focuses that help the children reread or look more closely at the text;
- encourage children to respond to their reading in a variety of ways.

Benefits of small group teaching and reading

Small group teaching and reading enables children to work in a small group with the teacher on a regular basis and be supported by the teacher as they independently read more challenging texts. The teacher is able to monitor closely the reading of each child and intervene when appropriate. The children are able to read and discuss their reading with a small number of other children who have the same text. Because of the size of the group, they are more able to share their responses to, and questions or discussions about, their reading.

Through working in small groups, the children will have more opportunities to interact with the teacher and their peers, and to be guided on specific reading skills, knowledge and responses.

Organisation for small group teaching and reading

Regular times for small group teaching and reading need to be included as part of the reading program. The approach outlined in this guide suggests that reading sessions be conducted every day, and that small group teaching and reading is an integral, predictable teaching procedure within each of these reading sessions. Each child will participate in small group teaching and reading at least once a week. For example, if there are four reading groups within the class this means that, over four reading sessions, all groups will have participated in small group teaching and reading. The fifth reading session is available for further needs-based teaching as required. Alternatively, if time allows, each child may participate in small group teaching and reading twice a week. For example, if there are four reading groups within the class, this means that during each session two groups will have participated in small group teaching and reading. The fifth session is still available for further needs-based teaching as required.

The weekly timetable

The weekly timetable below demonstrates two ways of organising small group teaching and reading involving four groups of children. When each teaching group is working with the teacher, the rest of the children are working independently of the teacher, in small groups or individually, on reading and other related activities.

Sometimes these activities will be related to the book they have been introduced to, have read or are reading in their small group or they may be completely unrelated. For the purposes of this guide, only the small group teaching and reading activities have been described.

Example of a weekly timetable for reading, involving one small group teaching session each day

	Mon	Tue	Wed	Thur	Fri
Purple group	Small group teaching and reading	Independent reading and response	Independent reading and response	Independent reading and response	Class working independently or in groups on individual or common reading and response activities. Teaching groups as required.
Yellow group	Independent reading and response	Small group teaching and reading	Independent reading and response	Independent reading and response	
Blue group	Independent reading and response	Independent reading and response	Small group teaching and reading	Independent reading and response	
Green group	Independent reading and response	Independent reading and response	Independent reading and response	Small group teaching and reading	

Example of a weekly timetable for reading, involving two small group teaching sessions each day

	Mon	Tue	Wed	Thur	Fri
Purple group	teacher / response	Independent reading and response	teacher / response	Independent reading and response	Class working independently or in groups on individual or common reading and response activities. Teaching groups as required.
Yellow group	independent / teacher	Independent reading and response	independent / teacher	Independent reading and response	
Blue group	Independent reading and response	teacher / response	Independent reading and response	teacher / response	
Green group	Independent reading and response	teacher / response	Independent reading and response	teacher / response	

The reading session plan

The reading session plans on the following pages demonstrate two ways of conducting a one-hour reading session. The first plan involves two groups participating in a small group teaching and reading procedure, while the second involves only one group. The session plans can be adapted to suit the teaching style of the teacher and the needs of the children.

Example of the structure of a reading session, involving two small group teaching sessions

10 minutes	**Whole class focus:** This is a focused teaching time. It may involve reading to or with the children. It will include the explicit teaching of a reading procedure or strategy.
15–20 minutes	**Small group teaching and reading:** A group of children with similar reading skills works with the teacher. → First target reading group works with teacher. Rest of class working independently or in groups on individual or common reading and response activities. → Independent or group reading and response. / Independent or group reading and response. / Independent or group reading and response.
15–20 minutes	Second target reading group works with teacher. Rest of class working independently or in groups on individual or common reading and response activities. → First group completes any reading or response work arising from working with the teacher. / Independent or group reading and response. / Independent or group reading and response.
5–10 minutes	**Sharetime:** This may include sharing responses, reflection, explicit teaching.

Example of the structure of a reading session, involving one small group teaching session

10–15 minutes	**Whole class focus:** This is a focused teaching time. It may involve reading to or with the children. It will include the explicit teaching of a reading procedure or strategy.	
30 minute	**Small group teaching and reading:** A group of children with similar reading skills works with the teacher.	Rest of class working independently or in groups on individual or common reading and response activities.
15–20 minutes	**Sharetime:** This may include sharing responses, reflection, explicit teaching.	

The procedure for small group teaching and reading sessions

The procedure for small group teaching and reading is predictable, and is designed to provide the children with successful reading experiences under the guidance of the teacher, who provides support at the point of need for each student. The procedure is described below:

Forming groups and selecting books

Books should be selected to cater for the children's reading and developmental needs. To assist the teacher to do this, a list of the features and teaching possibilities of each title appears at the beginning of the teachers' notes in this guide. The table on pp.12–15 indicates some of the text structures, features and literacy skills that could be focused upon for each title.

This information, plus the teacher's knowledge of the child gained from formal and informal reading assessment, will help the teacher decide the composition of each small group. The reading records included in this guide (see pp.23–24) may assist in the matching of texts to children. Each child must have their own copy of the book.

Deciding on the teaching and reading focus for each small group

It is advisable for the teacher to read through the notes for the selected book before working with each group. The teacher needs to be familiar with the challenges within the book and the approaches and supports that can be used to assist the children to read for meaning, improve their reading and thinking strategies, and develop varied and rich responses to their reading. The notes provide suggestions for specific focuses for each session.

The specific teaching focuses may include aspects of both literacy and literary teaching and learning. They may involve the exploration of, for example:

- levels of meaning;
- the writer's craft;
- text structure and language features;
- responses to reading.

Preparing for reading

Assist the children to prepare for independent reading of the book by:

- encouraging them to look at the book and its parts, and asking them to predict what the book might be about;
- talking about the topic of the book and relating this to their own experiences and knowledge;
- predicting, listing and using the vocabulary and grammatical structures that appear in the book;
- providing essential knowledge (such as concepts, vocabulary, author background, and text structure) that may assist the children's understanding of the book or section;
- modelling how to read, by reading a small part of the text aloud or demonstrating a specific reading strategy.

During independent reading

Set appropriate focus questions or discussion prompts. Encourage the children to read a nominated part of the book silently to find specific information and to prepare for discussion or response. As the children read, use the time to observe their reading behaviours and provide support and challenges as required.

Early finishers can be given other questions to explore as they wait for all children to complete their reading. During this part of the session, move among the children and observe their reading behaviours, assisting children as they require it.

After reading

Allow the children time to discuss the answers to the focus questions and to share their responses to what they have read. Help them to reflect on their reading skills and knowledge and help them to articulate what they do as readers, and what they find easy or difficult.

Encourage the children to think about and respond to their reading in many ways by providing questions and activities that require higher-level thinking skills. Select activities that require them to reread the text or to make connections beyond the text.

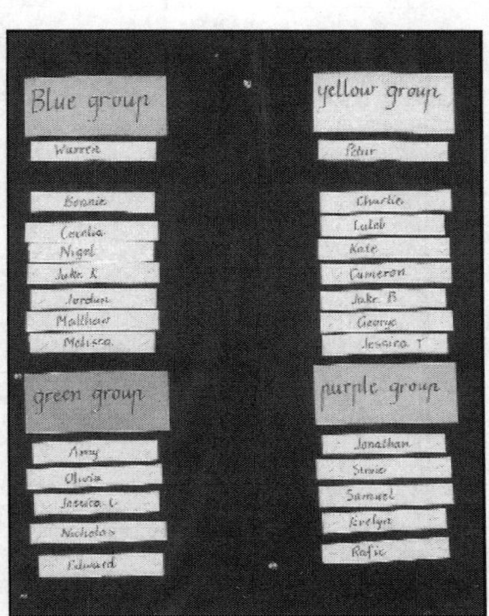

Checklist of text features and specific language skills

PM Library Emerald Level	Chapter Books – Set A						Chapter Books – Set B					
	Tall Tales	The Secret	The Falcon	Queen of the Pool	The Creature of Cassidy's Creek	MacTavish's Creature	The Trouble with Oatmeal	Super-Tuned!	The Junkyard Dog	The Crystal Unicorn	A Medal for Molly	Alfred the Curious
TEXT TYPES												
Diary												
Information report												
Interview												
Letter	*						*					
Narrative												
Mystery					*	*						
Realistic		*	*	*				*				*
Persuasive text												
Advertisement												
Argument												
Discussion												
Procedure												
Recount									*	*	*	
Verse												
TEXT STRUCTURES AND FEATURES												
Blurb												
Chapter headings		*	*	*		*	*	*	*	*	*	*
Diagrams												
Enlarged text							*					
Glossary												
Index												
Inserts												
Italics			*				*					
Labels												
Lists												
Sub-headings												
Table of contents		*	*	*	*	*	*	*	*	*	*	
Punctuation												
Apostrophe for contractions								*				
Apostrophe of possession											*	
Brackets												
Dashes		*					*					
Ellipsis					*		*					*

PM Non-fiction						PM Anthology: Funny Business											
Yo-yos	The Pushcart Team	Snowboarding Diary	Skateboarding	Kites	The Bicycle Book	10 things your parents will never say	Woof	Tidying my room	Reasons we can't get a dog	Digger reckons	Drawing Digger	The dangerous dinosaur	The school play	Funny business	Magnetic madness	Fruit	Buster and the balloon man
	*	*												*			
*	*	*	*	*	*	*								*			
											*						
			*														
							*										
								*		*			*		*	*	*
			*						*								
			*														
*	*			*	*												
	*	*								*							
								*				*					
*	*			*	*					*					*		
	*	*	*	*													
												*		*			
*	*	*	*	*	*												
*	*	*	*	*	*												
		*			*									*			
*							*			*			*			*	
	*			*	*												
	*			*													
*					*									*			
*																	
						*		*				*	*		*		
															*	*	
					*							*		*		*	
							*			*	*			*		*	
										*	*	*	*		*		

PM Library Emerald Level	Chapter Books – Set A						Chapter Books – Set B					
	Tall Tales	The Secret	The Falcon	Queen of the Pool	The Creature of Cassidy's Creek	MacTavish's Creature	The Trouble with Oatmeal	Super-Tuned!	The Junkyard Dog	The Crystal Unicorn	A Medal for Molly	Alfred the Curious
TEXT STRUCTURES AND FEATURES continued												
Exclamation marks							*	*				
Hyphens								*				
Inverted commas							*					
Question marks												
Speech marks			*	*			*	*	*	*		
Adjectives			*			*						*
Adverbs					*							
Verbs			*	*					*			*
Conjunctions								*				
Nouns		*										
Prepositions					*							
Pronouns		*							*	*		
Abbreviations							*					
Compound words												
Homophones												
Metaphors												
Onomatopoeic words												*
Prefixes										*		
Similes												
Specialised or subject-specific vocabulary												*
Suffixes							*					
Synonyms		*				*		*				
Word endings							*					
SPECIFIC LITERACY SKILLS												
Using the dictionary		*	*				*			*	*	
Using the thesaurus		*										
Identifying inferred meaning	*								*		*	
Identifying literal meaning	*	*	*	*	*	*	*	*	*	*	*	*
Identifying cause and effect								*		*	*	*
Thinking beyond the text	*	*	*	*	*	*	*	*	*	*	*	*
Identifying character traits		*				*						
Forming open and closed questions	*											
ICT SKILLS												
File management	*	*	*	*	*	*	*	*	*	*	*	*
Graphics		*			*	*	*	*			*	
Multimedia		*				*						
Word processing	*		*	*	*		*	*	*	*	*	*
Electronic communication			*									*

	PM Non-fiction						PM Anthology: Funny Business											
	Yo-yos	The Pushcart Team	Snowboarding Diary	Skateboarding	Kites	The Bicycle Book	10 things your parents will never say	Woof	Tidying my room	Reasons we can't get a dog	Digger reckons	Drawing Digger	The dangerous dinosaur	The school play	Funny business	Magnetic madness	Fruit	Buster and the balloon man
							*	*		*	*	*	*	*	*	*	*	*
			*				*						*					*
	*														*			
							*			*	*	*		*	*		*	
		*						*			*			*		*	*	*
								*	*	*			*	*		*	*	
				*					*			*						
									*					*				
			*	*														
					*													
				*														
	*				*													
												*						
	*	*	*		*	*												
	*			*	*	*												
												*						
	*	*	*	*	*	*	*	*	*	*	*	*	*	*	*	*	*	*
			*			*												
	*		*	*	*	*	*	*	*	*	*	*	*	*	*	*	*	*
								*										
	*	*	*	*	*	*									*			
	*	*			*										*			
	*																	
			*	*		*												
			*	*														

Using the teachers' notes in this guide

Content of the teacher's notes

The teachers' notes provide suggestions for the use of each book in small groups of children with similar reading abilities and needs (target groups).

Each set of teachers' notes includes:

- a short **synopsis** of the content;
- suggested **activities** for two teaching sessions with a target group, during which the teacher guides the children to read for meaning and to develop appropriate reading strategies and responses;
- suggested **focuses** for one or more **independent reading sessions**, during which the children complete the reading of the book;
- three **blackline masters** which are designed to focus the children's attention on and provide practice in specific reading, writing and ICT skills and knowledge.

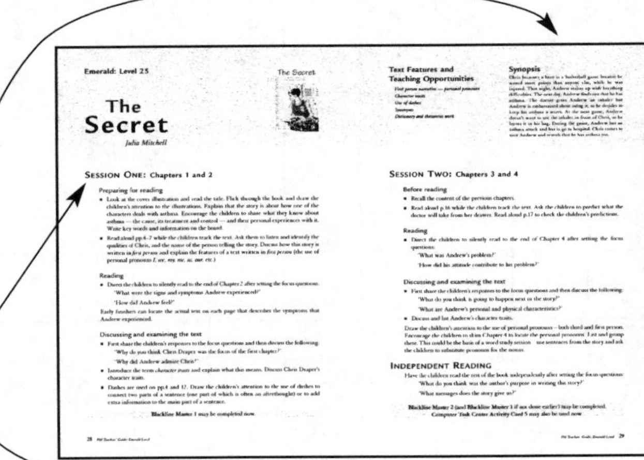

Emerald: Level 25

The Secret

Julia Mitchell

Text Features and Teaching Opportunities

Synopsis

SESSION ONE: Chapters 1 and 2

SESSION TWO: Chapters 3 and 4

INDEPENDENT READING

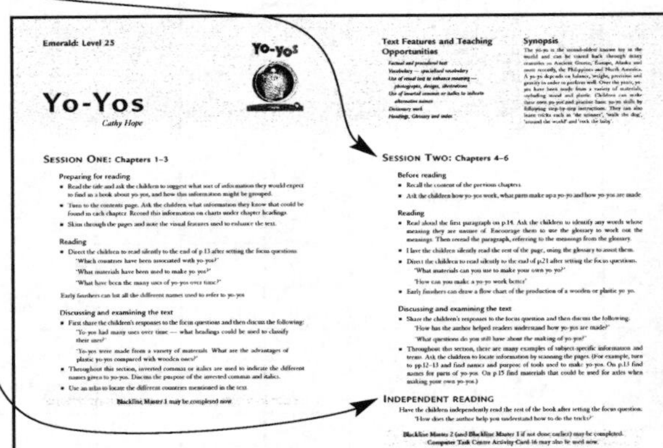

Emerald: Level 25

Yo-Yos

Cathy Hope

Text Features and Teaching Opportunities

Synopsis

SESSION ONE: Chapters 1–3

SESSION TWO: Chapters 4–6

INDEPENDENT READING

The **first blackline master** for each title can be used between the first and second small group reading session or at the completion of the book. When and if it is used is dependent on the teacher's purpose and the needs of the children.

The **second blackline master** is designed to be used at the completion of the reading of the book.

The **third blackline master** is a **computer task centre activity card.** There is a computer task centre activity card for each book at Emerald Level and generic cards that would be suitable to use with any book. The cards have been written to be used at the computer learning centre so that information and communication technology skills (or ICT skills) can be developed in the context of a language activity related to one of the books. The cards are designed for independent work or for students to work in pairs, perhaps with peer tutoring. The cards can be laminated, put in plastic sleeves or mounted on card and attached to computers with Blu-tack.

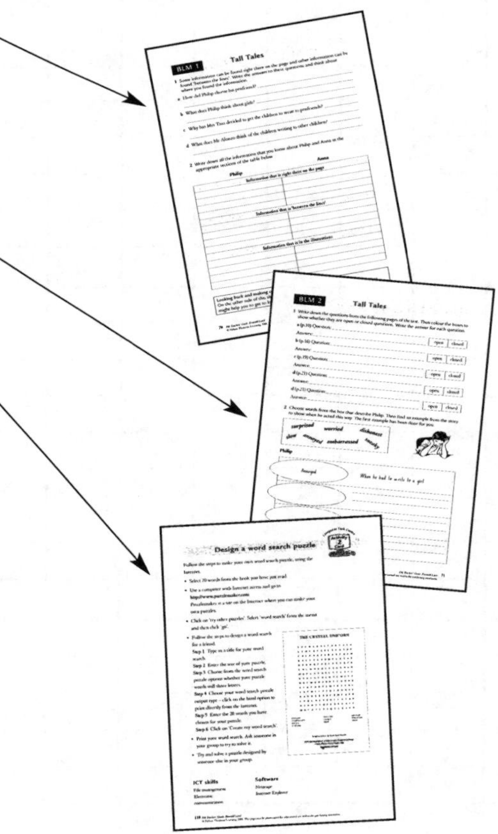

BLM 1 Tall Tales

BLM 2 Tall Tales

Design a word search puzzle

Format of teachers' notes for each small group teaching session

The teachers' notes include the same format for two small group teaching and reading sessions.

1 Preparing for reading

This section contains suggestions for ways that teachers can prepare the children for reading a particular book. Preparation for reading will involve identifying and building on the children's prior knowledge of the subject of the book, and discussing the text structure and language features.

2 Reading

There are suggested focus questions to help the children with silent reading of the designated section of the book. These focus questions can be written on the board or where children can easily refer to them. The focus questions are designed to help children interact with and think about the text in a variety of ways. There are suggestions for authentic reading or response work for early finishers to do, while waiting for the rest of the group to finish reading.

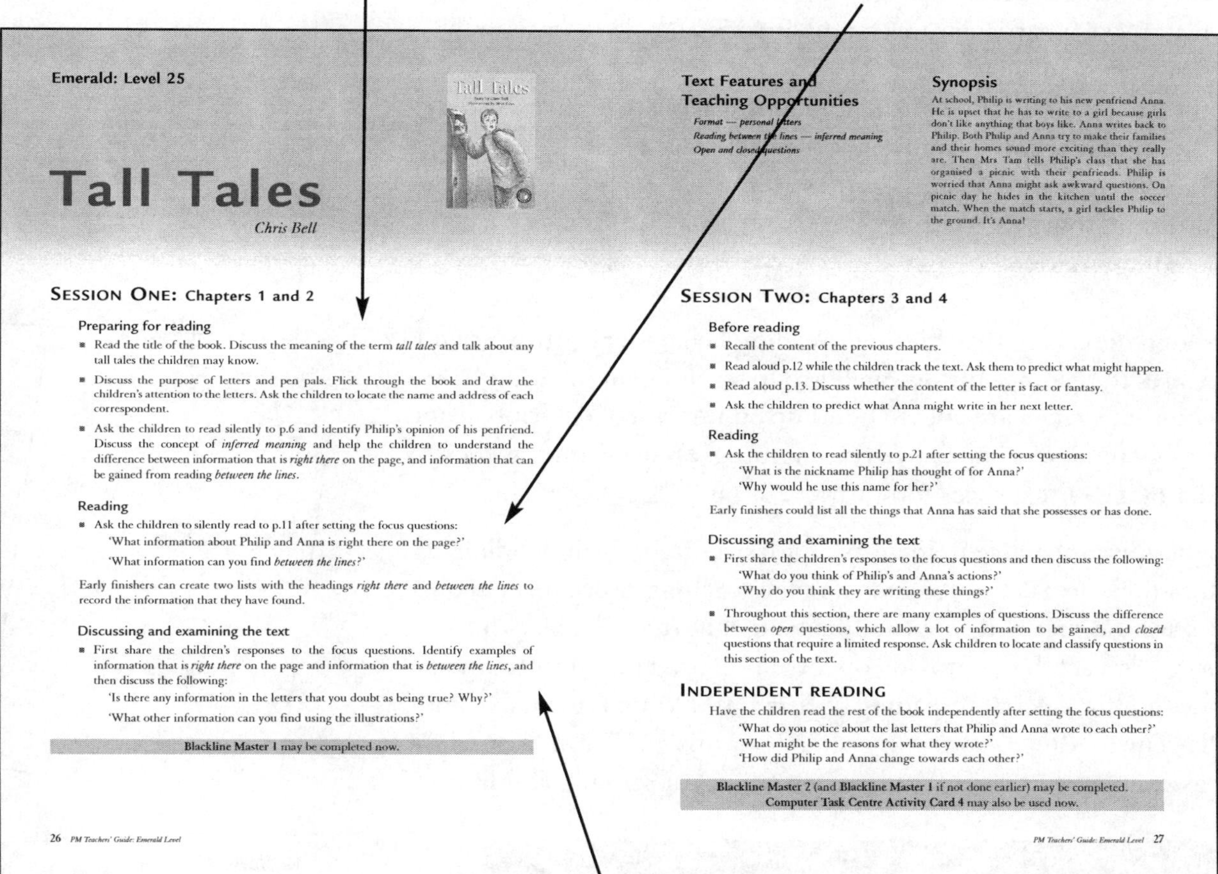

Emerald: Level 25

Tall Tales

Chris Bell

Text Features and Teaching Opportunities

Format — personal letters
Reading between the lines — inferred meaning
Open and closed questions

Synopsis

At school, Philip is writing to his new penfriend Anna. He is upset that he has to write to a girl because girls don't like anything that boys like. Anna writes back to Philip. Both Philip and Anna try to make their families and their homes sound more exciting than they really are. Then Mrs Tam tells Philip's class that she has organised a picnic with their penfriends. Philip is worried that Anna might ask awkward questions. On picnic day he hides in the kitchen until the soccer match. When the match starts, a girl tackles Philip to the ground. It's Anna!

SESSION ONE: Chapters 1 and 2

Preparing for reading

- Read the title of the book. Discuss the meaning of the term *tall tales* and talk about any tall tales the children may know.
- Discuss the purpose of letters and pen pals. Flick through the book and draw the children's attention to the letters. Ask the children to locate the name and address of each correspondent.
- Ask the children to read silently to p.6 and identify Philip's opinion of his penfriend. Discuss the concept of *inferred meaning* and help the children to understand the difference between information that is *right there* on the page, and information that can be gained from reading *between the lines*.

Reading

- Ask the children to silently read to p.11 after setting the focus questions:
  'What information about Philip and Anna is right there on the page?'
  'What information can you find *between the lines*?'

Early finishers can create two lists with the headings *right there* and *between the lines* to record the information that they have found.

Discussing and examining the text

- First share the children's responses to the focus questions. Identify examples of information that is *right there* on the page and information that is *between the lines*, and then discuss the following:
  'Is there any information in the letters that you doubt as being true? Why?'
  'What other information can you find using the illustrations?'

Blackline Master 1 may be completed now.

26 *PM Teachers' Guide: Emerald Level*

SESSION TWO: Chapters 3 and 4

Before reading

- Recall the content of the previous chapters.
- Read aloud p.12 while the children track the text. Ask them to predict what might happen.
- Read aloud p.13. Discuss whether the content of the letter is fact or fantasy.
- Ask the children to predict what Anna might write in her next letter.

Reading

- Ask the children to read silently to p.21 after setting the focus questions:
  'What is the nickname Philip has thought of for Anna?'
  'Why would he use this name for her?'

Early finishers could list all the things that Anna has said that she possesses or has done.

Discussing and examining the text

- First share the children's responses to the focus questions and then discuss the following:
  'What do you think of Philip's and Anna's actions?'
  'Why do you think they are writing these things?'
- Throughout this section, there are many examples of questions. Discuss the difference between *open* questions, which allow a lot of information to be gained, and *closed* questions that require a limited response. Ask children to locate and classify questions in this section of the text.

INDEPENDENT READING

Have the children read the rest of the book independently after setting the focus questions:
'What do you notice about the last letters that Philip and Anna wrote to each other?'
'What might be the reasons for what they wrote?'
'How did Philip and Anna change towards each other?'

Blackline Master 2 (and **Blackline Master 1** if not done earlier) may be completed.
Computer Task Centre Activity Card 4 may also be used now.

PM Teachers' Guide: Emerald Level 27

3 Discussing and examining the text

There are further questions and prompts to stimulate group discussion, and to assist the children to respond to their reading in many ways, taking them beyond the text. The questions and discussion prompts are designed to help children think in different ways and provide responses that require higher level thinking. For example, children may be required to think creatively, critically and analytically. They may have to recall or rephrase information, to compare and contrast, list and describe, link cause and effect, put together or pull apart information or form opinions. Different types of questions (open, closed, rhetorical) are used for different purposes.

Assessment

Monitoring student reading progress

Assessment of children's reading development should be regular and ongoing, and should inform planning and the selection of texts at the appropriate level. Small group teaching and reading sessions are excellent contexts for monitoring individual students' reading in relation to the following:

- the range of text types read;
- the students' understanding of the context, purpose and audience for particular texts;
- the reading strategies used;
- the students' understanding of the structures and language features of a particular text, and how this knowledge is used to assist reading;
- the quality and range of the students' responses to their reading;
- the students' understanding of themselves as readers;
- knowledge of the reading process;
- attitudes towards reading;
- reading interests.

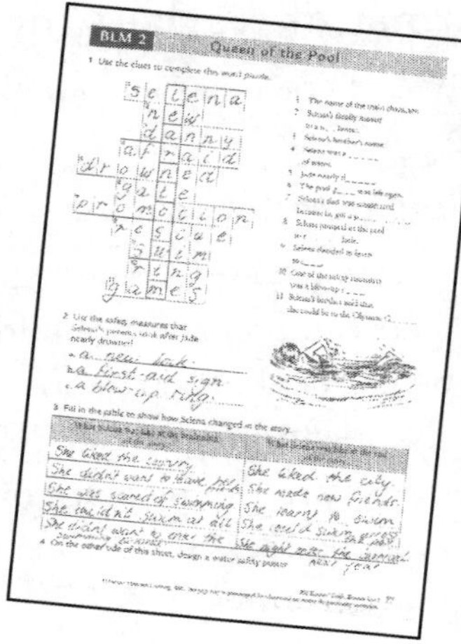
BLM 2 Queen of the Pool

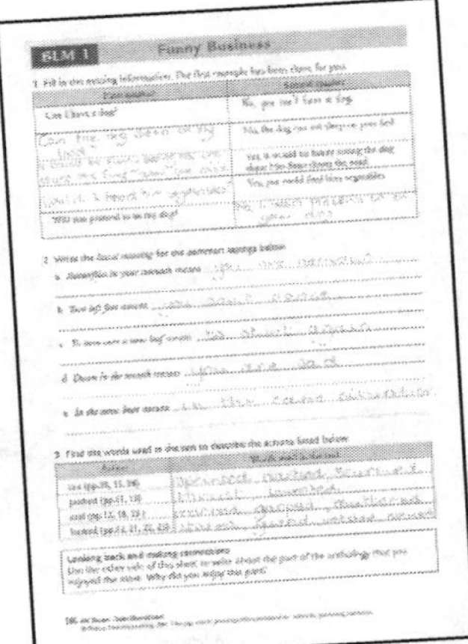
BLM 1 Funny Business

Through observing the children's reading behaviours, attitudes and responses to reading during small group teaching and reading situations, teachers are able to build up an informed, descriptive and rich assessment of each child's reading progress over time, as they read a range of text types for a variety of purposes.

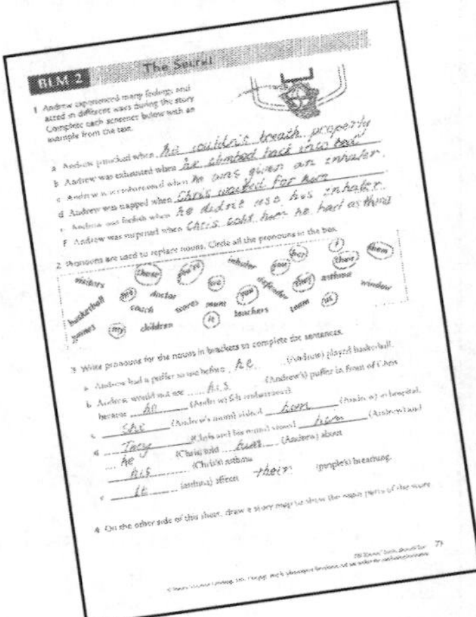
BLM 2 The Secret

Teachers are then able to identify children's strengths in reading, as well as their areas of need, and can plan teaching procedures and text selection that will support or extend children. The blackline masters for each book provide opportunities to gather information about specific aspects of reading, writing, thinking, knowledge and skills. The reading records on pp.23–24 of this guide can be used for the assessment of specific reading behaviours of selected children.

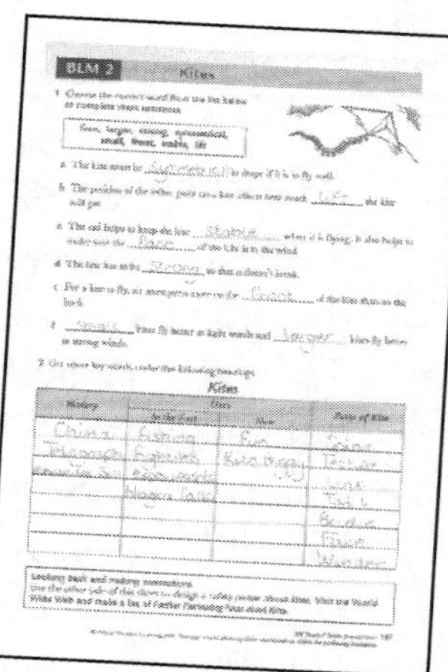
BLM 2 Kites

Assessment procedures and records

Both formal and informal assessment procedures may be used to monitor children's progress. Apart from the procedures used in the small group teaching and reading sessions, the teacher can use a range of procedures to assess and record the children's reading progress.

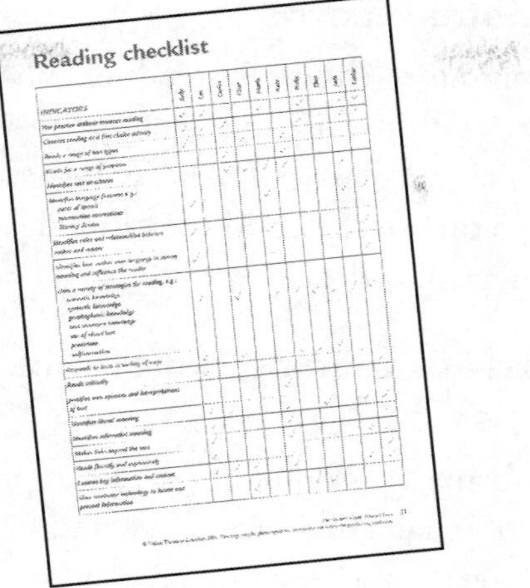
Reading checklist

Reading portfolios

These are collections of work and records of reading behaviours. Completed and annotated blackline masters associated with the books read can be stored in each child's portfolio, along with other reading related work (such as self-assessments, reading checklists, reading records [see pp.21–24], cloze activities, retellings, comprehension activities, prior- and post-reading knowledge and skills, concept maps, continuums, lists of books read, and directed reading thinking activities).

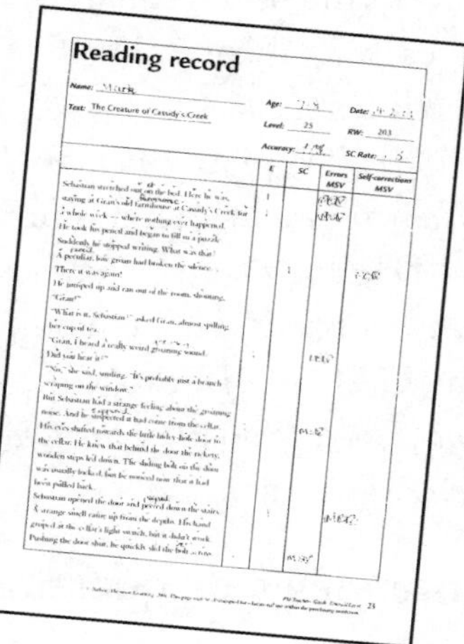
Reading record

Text: The Creature of Cassidy's Creek

Teacher-devised checklists

These can be made in advance of the small group teaching and reading sessions and can focus on the reading skills, knowledge, responses and attitudes to be assessed. As the children demonstrate particular behaviours, a tick can be placed beside their names.

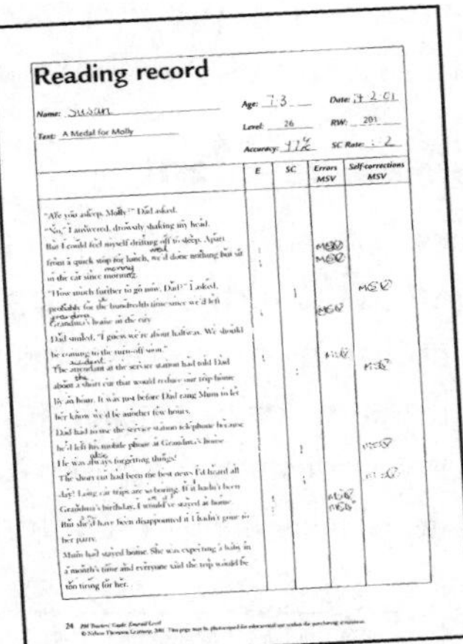
Reading record

Text: A Medal for Molly

Anecdotal records

Observations of children's reading behaviours can be recorded with the date and context in which the behaviour was observed. Anecdotal records provide a broad picture of the child's reading development in chronological order.

Records of reading behaviours and miscue analysis

These formal assessment procedures provide a clear record of what a child can read, and help teachers to match texts to the learning level of the child. The information from the miscue analysis helps teachers plan specific teaching focuses. For further information on these procedures see:

- Clay, M. 1991, *Becoming Literate: The Construction of Inner Control*, Heinemann, Portsmouth;
- Clay, M. 1993, *An Observation Survey of Early Literacy Achievement*, Heinemann, Auckland;
- Goodman, G.M. and Burke, C.L. 1972, *Reading Miscue Inventory: Procedure for Diagnosis and Evaluation*, Macmillan, London.

Reading interviews or questionnaires

Reading interviews or questionnaires, either completed orally or in written form, provide specific information about the child's reading behaviours and attitudes.

Student self-assessment

Student self-assessment provides valuable information and insights into the children's perceptions of their reading. The children can record this information in many different ways, for example, oral reports, checklists, rating scales, reading journals, learning logs, continuums and pictorial representation (see p.22).

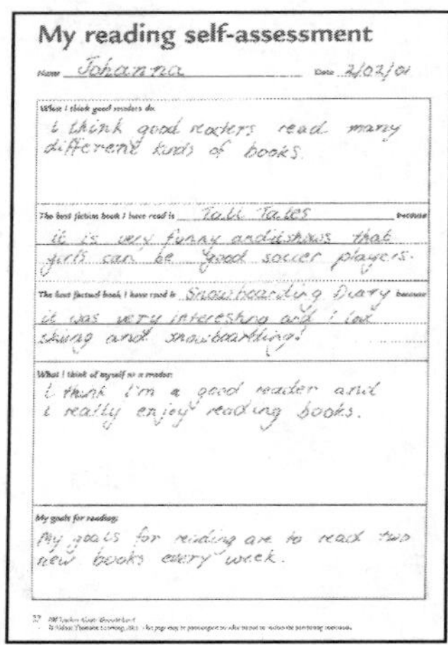

My reading self-assessment

Name Johanna Date 2/02/01

What I think good readers do:
I think good readers read many different kinds of books.

The best fiction book I have read is Tall Tales because
it is very funny and shows that girls can be good soccer players.

The best factual book I have read is Snowboarding Diary because
it was very interesting and I love skiing and snowboarding!

What I think of myself as a reader:
I think I'm a good reader and I really enjoy reading books.

My goals for reading:
My goals for reading are to read two new books every week.

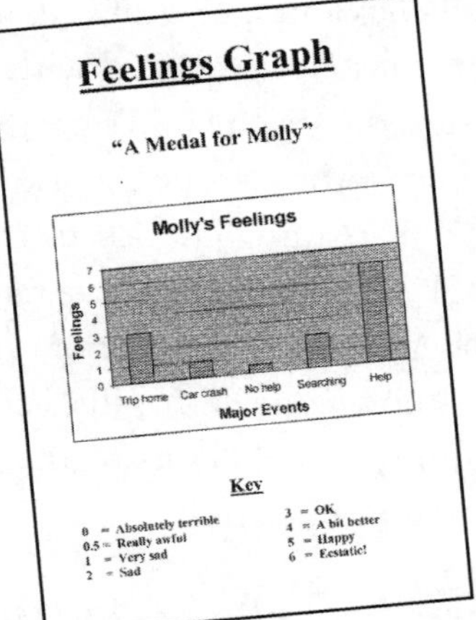

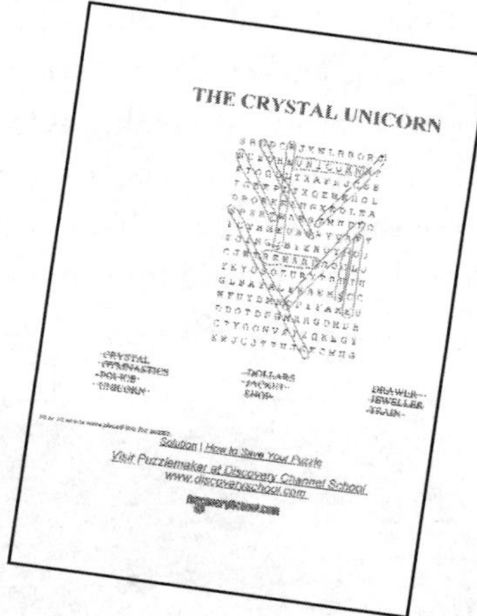

Reading checklist

INDICATORS										
Has positive attitude towards reading										
Chooses reading as a free choice activity										
Reads a range of text types										
Reads for a range of purposes										
Identifies text structures										
Identifies language features e.g.: *parts of speech* *punctuation conventions* *literary devices*										
Identifies roles and relationships between author and reader										
Identifies how author uses language to convey meaning and influence the reader										
Uses a variety of strategies for reading, e.g.: *semantic knowledge* *syntactic knowledge* *graphophonic knowledge* *text structure knowledge* *use of visual text* *prediction* *self-correction*										
Responds to texts in a variety of ways										
Reads critically										
Justifies own opinions and interpretations of text										
Identifies literal meaning										
Identifies inferential meaning										
Makes links beyond the text										
Reads fluently and expressively										
Locates key information and content										
Uses computer technology to locate and present information										

My reading self-assessment

Name ________________________________ ***Date*** ________________

What I think good readers do:

The best fiction book I have read is ____________________________ ***because***

The best factual book I have read is ____________________________ ***because***

What I think of myself as a reader:

My goals for reading:

Reading record

Name: ________________		**_Age:_** ________		**_Date:_** ________	
Text: The Creature of Cassidy's Creek		**_Level:_** 25		**_RW:_** 203	
		Accuracy: ________		**_SC Rate:_** ________	

	E	***SC***	***Errors MSV***	***Self-corrections MSV***
Sebastian stretched out on the bed. Here he was, staying at Gran's old farmhouse at Cassidy's Creek for a whole week — where nothing ever happened. He took his pencil and began to fill in a puzzle. Suddenly he stopped writing. What was that? A peculiar, low groan had broken the silence… There it was again! He jumped up and ran out of the room, shouting, "Gran!" "What is it, Sebastian?" asked Gran, almost spilling her cup of tea. "Gran, I heard a really weird groaning sound. Did you hear it?" "No," she said, smiling. "It's probably just a branch scraping on the window." But Sebastian had a strange feeling about the groaning noise. And he suspected it had come from the cellar. His eyes shifted towards the little hidey-hole door to the cellar. He knew that behind the door the rickety, wooden steps led down. The sliding bolt on the door was usually locked, but he noticed now that it had been pulled back. Sebastian opened the door and peered down the stairs. A strange smell came up from the depths. His hand groped at the cellar's light switch, but it didn't work. Pushing the door shut, he quickly slid the bolt across.				

Reading record

Name: ______________________ *Age:* __________ *Date:* __________

Text: A Medal for Molly *Level:* 26 *RW:* 201

Accuracy: __________ *SC Rate:* __________

	E	*SC*	*Errors MSV*	*Self-corrections MSV*
"Are you asleep, Molly?" Dad asked.				
"No," I answered, drowsily shaking my head.				
But I could feel myself drifting off to sleep. Apart from a quick stop for lunch, we'd done nothing but sit in the car since morning.				
"How much further to go now, Dad?" I asked, probably for the hundredth time since we'd left Grandma's house in the city.				
Dad smiled, "I guess we're about halfway. We should be coming to the turn-off soon."				
The attendant at the service station had told Dad about a short cut that would reduce our trip home by an hour. It was just before Dad rang Mum to let her know we'd be another few hours.				
Dad had to use the service station telephone because he'd left his mobile phone at Grandma's house.				
He was always forgetting things!				
The short cut had been the best news I'd heard all day! Long car trips are so boring. If it hadn't been Grandma's birthday, I would've stayed at home.				
But she'd have been disappointed if I hadn't gone to her party.				
Mum had stayed home. She was expecting a baby in a month's time and everyone said the trip would be too tiring for her.				

Teachers' notes for the books at Emerald Level

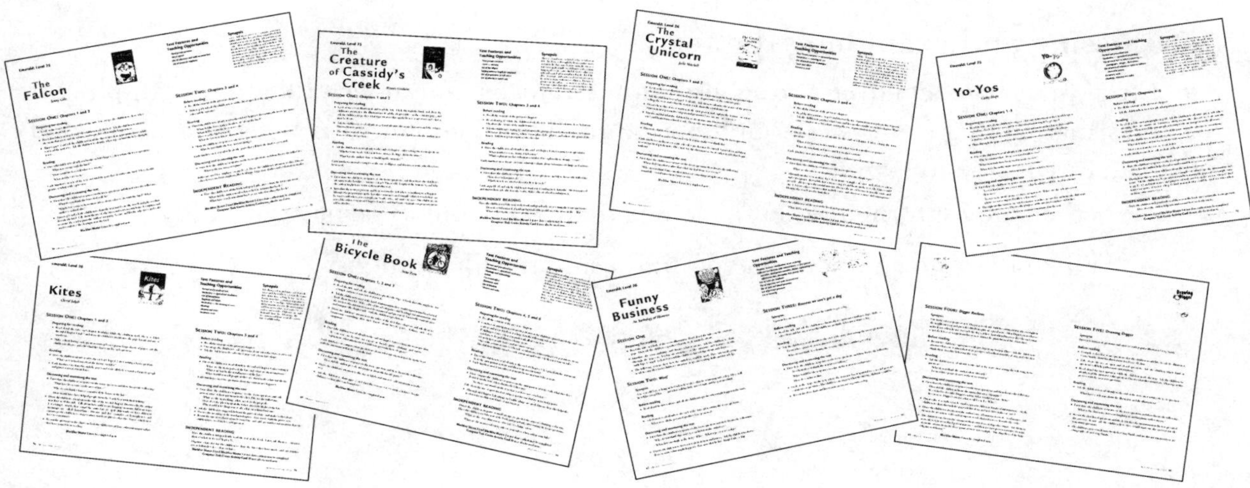

Emerald: Level 25

Tall Tales

Chris Bell

SESSION ONE: Chapters 1 and 2

Preparing for reading

- Read the title of the book. Discuss the meaning of the term *tall tales* and talk about any tall tales the children may know.
- Discuss the purpose of letters and pen pals. Flick through the book and draw the children's attention to the letters. Ask the children to locate the name and address of each correspondent.
- Ask the children to read silently to p.6 and identify Philip's opinion of his penfriend. Discuss the concept of *inferred meaning* and help the children to understand the difference between information that is *right there* on the page, and information that can be gained from reading *between the lines*.

Reading

- Ask the children to silently read to p.11 after setting the focus questions:

  'What information about Philip and Anna is right there on the page?'

  'What information can you find *between the lines*?'

Early finishers can create two lists with the headings *right there* and *between the lines* to record the information that they have found.

Discussing and examining the text

- First share the children's responses to the focus questions. Identify examples of information that is *right there* on the page and information that is *between the lines*, and then discuss the following:

  'Is there any information in the letters that you doubt as being true? Why?'

  'What other information can you find using the illustrations?'

Blackline Master 1 may be completed now.

Text Features and Teaching Opportunities

Format — personal letters
Reading between the lines — inferred meaning
Open and closed questions

Synopsis

At school, Philip is writing to his new penfriend Anna. He is upset that he has to write to a girl because girls don't like anything that boys like. Anna writes back to Philip. Both Philip and Anna try to make their families and their homes sound more exciting than they really are. Then Mrs Tam tells Philip's class that she has organised a picnic with their penfriends. Philip is worried that Anna might ask awkward questions. On picnic day he hides in the kitchen until the soccer match. When the match starts, a girl tackles Philip to the ground. It's Anna!

SESSION TWO: Chapters 3 and 4

Before reading

- Recall the content of the previous chapters.
- Read aloud p.12 while the children track the text. Ask them to predict what might happen.
- Read aloud p.13. Discuss whether the content of the letter is fact or fantasy.
- Ask the children to predict what Anna might write in her next letter.

Reading

- Ask the children to read silently to p.21 after setting the focus questions:
  'What is the nickname Philip has thought of for Anna?'
  'Why would he use this name for her?'

Early finishers could list all the things that Anna has said that she possesses or has done.

Discussing and examining the text

- First share the children's responses to the focus questions and then discuss the following:
  'What do you think of Philip's and Anna's actions?'
  'Why do you think they are writing these things?'
- Throughout this section, there are many examples of questions. Discuss the difference between *open* questions, which allow a lot of information to be gained, and *closed* questions that require a limited response. Ask children to locate and classify questions in this section of the text.

INDEPENDENT READING

Have the children read the rest of the book independently after setting the focus questions:

'What do you notice about the last letters that Philip and Anna wrote to each other?'
'What might be the reasons for what they wrote?'
'How did Philip and Anna change towards each other?'

Blackline Master 2 (and **Blackline Master 1** if not done earlier) may be completed.
Computer Task Centre Activity Card 4 may also be used now.

Emerald: Level 25

The Secret

Julia Mitchell

Session One: Chapters 1 and 2

Preparing for reading

- Look at the cover illustration and read the title. Flick through the book and draw the children's attention to the illustrations. Explain that the story is about how one of the characters deals with asthma. Encourage the children to share what they know about asthma — the cause, its treatment and control — and their personal experiences with it. Write key words and information on the board.
- Read aloud pp.4–7 while the children track the text. Ask them to listen and identify the qualities of Chris, and the name of the person telling the story. Discuss how this story is written in *first person* and explain the features of a text written in *first person* (the use of personal pronouns *I, we, my, me, us, our,* etc.).

Reading

- Direct the children to read silently to the end of Chapter 2 after setting the focus questions:

  'What were the signs and symptoms Andrew experienced?'

  'How did Andrew feel?'

Early finishers can locate the actual text on each page that describes the symptoms that Andrew experienced.

Discussing and examining the text

- First share the children's responses to the focus questions and then discuss the following:

  'Why do you think Chris Draper was the focus of the first chapter?'

  'Why did Andrew admire Chris?'

- Introduce the term *character traits* and explain what this means. Discuss Chris Draper's character traits.
- Dashes are used on pp.4 and 12. Draw the children's attention to the use of dashes to connect two parts of a sentence (one part of which is often an afterthought) or to add extra information to the main part of a sentence.

Blackline Master 1 may be completed now.

Text Features and Teaching Opportunities

First person narrative — personal pronouns
Character traits
Use of dashes
Synonyms
Dictionary and thesaurus work

Synopsis

Chris becomes a hero in a basketball game because he scored more points than anyone else, while he was injured. That night, Andrew wakes up with breathing difficulties. The next day, Andrew finds out that he has asthma. The doctor gives Andrew an inhaler but Andrew is embarrassed about using it, so he decides to keep his asthma a secret. At the next game, Andrew doesn't want to use the inhaler in front of Chris, so he leaves it in his bag. During the game, Andrew has an asthma attack and has to go to hospital. Chris comes to visit Andrew and reveals that he has asthma too.

SESSION TWO: Chapters 3 and 4

Before reading

- Recall the content of the previous chapters.
- Read aloud p.16 while the children track the text. Ask the children to predict what the doctor will take from her drawer. Read aloud p.17 to check the children's predictions.

Reading

- Direct the children to read silently to the end of Chapter 4 after setting the focus questions:

  'What was Andrew's problem?'

  'How did his attitude contribute to his problem?'

Discussing and examining the text

- First share the children's responses to the focus questions and then discuss the following:

  'What do you think is going to happen next in the story?'

  'What are Andrew's personal and physical characteristics?'

- Discuss and list Andrew's character traits.

Draw the children's attention to the use of personal pronouns – both third and first person. Encourage the children to skim Chapter 4 to locate the personal pronouns. List and group these. This could be the basis of a word study session – use sentences from the story and ask the children to substitute pronouns for the nouns.

INDEPENDENT READING

Have the children read the rest of the book independently after setting the focus questions:

'What do you think was the author's purpose in writing this story?'

'What messages does the story give us?'

Blackline Master 2 (and **Blackline Master 1** if not done earlier) may be completed.
Computer Task Centre Activity Card 5 may also be used now.

Emerald: Level 25

The Falcon

Stephen Harrison

Session One: Chapters 1 and 2

Preparing for reading

- Look at the cover illustration and read the title. Encourage the children to share what they know about falcons.
- Read aloud the text on p.4 while the children track the text. Ask the children to identify the main characters and the setting, and to predict what might happen next.
- Turn to pp.6–7 and ask the children to read the direct speech at appropriate times while you read the narrative. Ask the children to identify what type of bird the boys thought it was.

Reading

- Direct the children to read silently to the end of Chapter 2 after setting the focus questions:

  'What was wrong with the bird?'

  'How could the boys tell what was wrong?'

  'What did they try to do?'

Early finishers can reread the text and find the part that describes the bird. They should practise reading with expression.

Discussing and examining the text

- First share the children's responses to the focus questions and then discuss the following:

  'What do you think the boys' dad will do?'

  'Which boy seems to have more ideas about what to do with the bird? What makes you think this?'
- Turn to p.8 and ask the children to skim the text and locate the words and phrases that describe the bird. Talk about the use of adjectives and verbs to enrich the description and to ensure the reader gains the author's meaning. Locate and list the adjectives and verbs used to enhance the description of the bird.

Blackline Master 1 may be completed now.

Text Features and Teaching Opportunities

Third person narrative
Direct speech
Use of adjectives and verbs to enrich text
Use of italics for emphasis

Synopsis

Carlos and Ricky arrive at a campsite with their father, where they discover a large injured bird. Dad identifies it as a falcon and he calls a nearby rescue centre. Max and Lisa, from the Raptor Centre, put the falcon in a cage and take it back with them. The falcon does well and Max suggests the boys come to watch the release of the falcon in a few weeks. Later, the boys and their parents go to the place where the bird will be released. Their father tells them they should feel proud about helping to save the falcon, which flies off into the distance.

Session Two: Chapters 3 and 4

Before reading

- Recall the content of the previous chapters.
- Turn to p.14 and ask the children to read the direct speech at the appropriate times while you read the narrative.

Reading

- Direct the children to read silently to the end of Chapter 4 after setting the focus questions:
  'What did the boys' father decide to do about the bird?'
  'What did he warn the boys not to do?'
  'How was the bird rescued?'
  'What do you now know about the bird?'
- Share the children's responses to the focus questions and then discuss the following:
  'Why do you think the boys weren't hungry?

Early finishers may reread to locate the parts that tell how the bird was rescued.

Discussing and examining the text

- First share the children's responses to the focus questions and then discuss the following:
  'What is the meaning of *raptor?*'

Italics are used for emphasis on pp.20–21. Draw the children's attention to this. Discuss other devices used for emphasis, like bold type, large font, dashes and exclamation marks.

Independent Reading

- Have the children read the book independently after setting the focus questions:
  'What did the author need to know before writing this book?'
  'What have you learnt about birds as a result of reading this book?'

Blackline Master 2 (and **Blackline Master 1** if not done earlier) may be completed.
Computer Task Centre Activity Card 6 may also be used now.

Emerald: Level 25

Queen of the Pool

Jan Weeks

SESSION ONE: Chapters 1 and 2

Preparing for reading

- Look at the cover illustration and read the title. Flick through the book and draw the children's attention to the illustrations. Read the chapter titles on the contents page and encourage the children to predict what the story might be about.
- Introduce the term *realistic fiction* and explain what this means. Discuss and compare the features of realistic fiction with those of fantasy.
- Read aloud pp.4–5 to the children and ask them to identify the key information.

Reading

- Have the children silently read Chapter 1 after setting the focus questions:

  'How did Selena feel about swimming?'

  'Why does she feel this way?'

  'Who has Selena met and how does she interact with them?'

Early finishers can list the people Selena has met.

Discussing and examining the text

- First share the children's responses to the focus questions and then discuss the following:

  'What do you now think will happen in the story?'

  'What do you think of Selena's parents' approach to her fear of swimming?'

Throughout this section there are examples of direct speech.

- Draw the children's attention to how this is written in present tense, while the rest of the text is in past tense. Discuss the reasons for this.
- Ask the children to skim the text and locate verbs that are written in the past or present tense. This could be the basis of a word study session.

Blackline Master 1 may be completed now.

Text Features and Teaching Opportunities

Third person narrative — use of past and present tense
Direct speech
Realistic fiction

Synopsis

Selena's family moves to a new home with a pool, but Selena is frightened of swimming. Her best friend Ellie has a baby sister, Jade. All the children enjoy the pool, but Selena won't go in. One day, Selena's family is babysitting Jade outside. Selena's mum goes inside and Danny follows her, leaving the pool gate open. Selena should be watching Jade but she falls asleep and wakes up to find that Jade has fallen into the pool. Selena rescues the baby and decides to learn how to swim. She learns new skills and feels very pleased that she is no longer afraid of the water.

SESSION TWO: Chapters 3 and 4

Before reading

- Recall the content of the previous chapters.
- Read the title of Chapter 3 and discuss its meaning.
- Read aloud pp.16–17 while the children track the text. Ask the children to predict what might happen next.

Reading

- Direct the children to read silently to the end of Chapter 4 after setting the focus questions:

  'What did Selena do to become a hero?'

  'What was the sequence of events that led to Selena's actions?'

Early finishers may locate, list and discuss the sequence of events that led to Selena's actions.

Discussing and examining the text

- First share the children's responses to the focus questions and then discuss the following:

  'Do you think Selena should have this label? Why?'

  'What were the safety measures the family put in place to prevent another accident?'

  'Who do you think was responsible for the accident? Why?'

INDEPENDENT READING

Have the children read the rest of the book independently after setting the focus questions:

'Why do you think the author chose this topic for a story?'

'This story is an example of realistic fiction. Which parts make it realistic? Which parts are similar to your own experiences?'

Blackline Master 2 (and **Blackline Master 1** if not done earlier) may be completed.
Computer Task Centre Activity Card 7 may also be used now.

Emerald: Level 25

The Creature of Cassidy's Creek

Wendy Graham

Session One: Chapters 1 and 2

Preparing for reading

- Look at the cover illustration and read the title. Flick through the book and draw the children's attention to the illustrations. Read the chapter titles on the contents page, and ask the children to predict what type of story this might be (i.e. a mystery) and what it may be about.
- Ask the children to read silently to p.4 and identify the main character and the setting. Discuss their responses.
- The ellipsis is used on p.4. Discuss its purpose and ask the children why the author may have used this device here.

Reading

- Ask the children to read silently to the end of Chapter 2 after setting the focus questions:

  'Which events made Sebastian have strange feelings about the noise?'

  'What has the author done to build up the suspense?'

Early finishers can find examples of the use of ellipses, and discuss or write why they have been used.

Discussing and examining the text

- First share the children's responses to the focus questions, and then draw the children's attention to the last three sentences on p.8. Discuss the length of the sentences, and why the author might have written them in this way.
- Introduce the term *preposition* and how it is used to tell where something is or happens. Identify the prepositions in the last three sentences and compile a list of words that can be used to tell where; for example, *on, beside, inside, up, under, in, over.* The children can reread the other sections of Chapters 1 and 2, and find more examples of prepositions to add to this list.

Blackline Master 1 may be completed now.

Text Features and Teaching Opportunities

Third person narrative
Genre — mystery
Use of the ellipsis
Varying sentence length for emphasis
Use of prepositions to tell where
Use of adverbs to enrich text

Synopsis

There's a weird noise in Gran's cellar, so Sebastian bolts the door. In the night he hears another noise, and finds the door ajar. Next morning, he notices a half-eaten apple, a spilt vase of flowers, and a curtain hanging off its rail. Later, the bolt on the cellar door is locked again, but Gran explains that she closed the door. Sebastian climbs a tree and sees movement in the front window of the house. Then he discovers a possum in the cellar. The mystery is solved, but Sebastian realises that while he was up in the tree the possum had been locked in the cellar — so what could the movement in the window have been? (The answer is revealed in the pictures on pp.19 and 32 — there is a second possum in the house!)

SESSION TWO: Chapters 3 and 4

Before reading

- Recall the content of the previous chapters.
- Read aloud p.12 while the children track the text. Ask them to identify how Sebastian felt about the events of the night before.
- Ask the children to skim p.12 and identify the groups of words that tell where Sebastian told Gran about the music, where Gran placed the plates, and where she poured the honey. Add these prepositions to the class list.

Reading

- Have the children read silently to the end of Chapter 4 after setting focus questions:
  'What further events alarmed Sebastian?'
  'What explanations has Sebastian considered to explain these strange events?'

Early finishers may discuss or write what they think about Sebastian's feelings and actions.

Discussing and examining the text

- First share the children's responses to the focus questions and then discuss the following:
  'How does Sebastian feel?'
  'Which words are used to describe how he feels?'

Look at pp.14–15 and ask the children to find words ending in *ly*. Introduce the term *adverb* and discuss how adverbs describe verbs. Make a list of adverbs ending in *ly*.

INDEPENDENT READING

Have the children read the rest of the book independently after setting the focus questions:

'How does Sebastian deal with and get rid of the problem of the noise in the cellar?'
'What still remains a mystery in this story?'

Blackline Master 2 (and **Blackline Master 1** if not done earlier) may be completed.
Computer Task Centre Activity Card 8 may also be used now.

Emerald: Level 25

MacTavish's Creature

Chris Bell

Session One: Chapters 1 and 2

Preparing for reading

- Look at the cover illustration and read the title. Read aloud the chapter titles on the contents page and then ask the children to predict what the story may be about.
- Talk about the name *MacTavish* and discuss what the children know about the origin of this name: for example, the country of origin and its associated customs.
- Ask the children to silently read pp.4–5 and identify the names of the first two characters, and what these characters are interested in.

Reading

- Direct the children to read silently to the end of Chapter 2 after setting the focus questions:

  'What events have made the boys really interested in the new neighbours and their possessions?'

  'What do you think the boys will do?'

Early finishers can share their predictions about what they think the boys will do and what might be making the noise.

Discussing and examining the text

- First share the children's responses to the focus questions and then discuss the following:

  'Which sentences in Chapter 2 indicate that the boys think there is something alive in the packing box?'

  'What do you think of the boys' first reactions to the new neighbours?'

  'How does the saying *don't judge a book by its cover* apply here?'

- The positive and comparative forms of an adjective are used on pp.4–5 of the text. Draw the children's attention to the use of the words *weird* and *weirder* and discuss the use of adjectives, introducing the terms *positive, comparative* and *superlative*. List the different forms of *weird* on a chart under the headings *positive, comparative* and *superlative*. Then ask the children to suggest other words that mean the same, for example:

peculiar *more peculiar* *most peculiar* *strange* *stranger* *strangest*

This could be the basis of a spelling or word study session.

Blackline Master 1 may be completed now.

Text Features and Teaching Opportunities

Third person narrative
Vocabulary — opportunities for development
Use of adjectives — positive, comparative and superlative

Synopsis

Alex and Brendan watch the new neighbours arrive and hear a loud groaning noise coming from a box marked 'fragile'. That night, Alex hears a wailing noise from next door. The next night, the boys camp out. When the noise starts they see the new neighbour, Dr MacTavish, wrestling with a strange creature. One night later, Alex trys to photograph Dr MacTavish with the creature, but Dr MacTavish grabs the boys and takes them inside. The boys explain that they thought Dr MacTavish had been torturing a creature. Dr MacTavish reveals the 'creature' — his bagpipes!

SESSION TWO: Chapters 3 and 4

Before reading

- Recall the content of the previous chapters.
- Read aloud p.17 while the children track the text, and ask them to identify how Brendan feels about the proposed actions. Encourage them to predict what they might see.
- Ask the children to silently read p.18 and locate what the boys did when they heard the noise.

Reading

- Direct the children to read silently to the end of Chapter 4 after setting the focus questions:

  'What did Mrs MacTavish say that convinced the boys that a living creature was making the noise?'

  'What was Dr MacTavish doing that concerned the boys?'

Early finishers may discuss, write or draw what they think will happen next.

Discussing and examining the text

- First share the children's responses to the focus questions and then discuss the following:

  'What do you think of the reactions of Alex's parents to the boys' story?'

  'What do you think Dr MacTavish will do to the boys?'

INDEPENDENT READING

Have the children read the rest of the book independently after setting the focus questions:

'What was the creature and why did it sound so bad?'

'What did Dr MacTavish think of the boys' explanation for their actions?'

Blackline Master 2 (and **Blackline Master 1** if not done earlier) may be completed.
Computer Task Centre Activity Card 9 may also be used now.

Emerald: Level 26

A Medal for Molly

Jan Weeks

Session One: Chapters 1 and 2

Preparing for reading

- Look at the cover illustration and read the title. Read aloud the chapter titles on the contents page and ask the children to predict what will happen in the story. List words and phrases the children suggest that are related to their predictions.
- Read aloud p.4 while the children track the text. Ask the children to listen for the part that tells how Molly feels.
- Draw the children's attention to the illustration on p.5. Talk about the children's experiences of long trips and their feelings.

Reading

- Direct the children to read silently to the end of Chapter 2 after setting the focus questions:

  'What do you know about the characters and the situation they are in?'

  'What caused the situation they are in?'

  'What makes their situation all the more difficult?'

Early finishers can locate the father's dialogue and practise reading this with expression.

Discussing and examining the text

- First share the children's responses to the focus questions and then discuss the following:

  'What information about the characters or the situation is not right there on the page, but rather *between the lines*?'

- Discuss the concept of inferred meaning and help the children to understand the difference between information that is *right there* on the page, and information that can be gained from reading *between the lines*. Help the children locate further examples of this.
- Discuss the concepts of cause and effect, and reason and action, and then ask the children how they would feel in this situation, and what they would do.

Blackline Master 1 may be completed now.

Text Features and Teaching Opportunities

First person recount
Reading between the lines — inferred meaning
Cause and effect
Apostrophe of possession
Dictionary work

Synopsis

Molly and her dad are driving home from Grandma's house. Molly falls asleep but wakes up when the car crashes. She is shaken, but Dad is trapped and passes out. Molly goes for help. She trudges through the rainy night and when dawn breaks, she sees a farmhouse. A woman takes Molly inside and calls an ambulance. She gives Molly dry clothes and a warm drink before they return to Molly's father. The ambulance is already there. A police officer tells Molly that she deserves a medal for bravery. But Molly is just glad that Dad is going to be alright.

SESSION TWO: Chapters 3 and 4

Before reading

- Recall the content of the previous chapters.
- Read aloud p.16 while the children track the text. Ask the children to listen for the three questions Molly poses. Discuss the children's responses to each of these questions.
- Read aloud p.17 and encourage the children to predict what Molly will do.

Reading

- Direct the children to read silently to the end of Chapter 4 after setting the focus questions:

  'What sort of difficulties did Molly have to overcome in order to help her dad?'

  'How would you describe Molly and her experiences?'

Early finishers may discuss or write words to describe Molly and her experiences.

Discussing and examining the text

- First share the children's responses to the focus questions and then discuss the following:

  'What does Molly do to help herself overcome her fears?'

  'What part on p.25 describes how she felt?'

Throughout this section are further examples of inferred meaning.

- Review the concept of finding information *between the lines* rather than information that is *right there* on the page. Help the children locate more examples of this.

INDEPENDENT READING

Have the children read independently to the end of the book after setting the focus questions:

'What was the sequence of events that concluded with Molly talking to the police officer?'

'Why did the author select this title for the book?'

Blackline Master 2 (and **Blackline Master 1** if not done earlier) may be completed.
Computer Task Centre Activity Card 10 may also be used now.

Emerald: Level 26

The Trouble with Oatmeal

Janet Slater Bottin

SESSION ONE: Chapters 1, 2 and 3

Preparing for reading

- Look at the cover and read the title. Flick through the book and show the children the illustrations. Read the contents and ask the children what the story may be about.
- Ask the children to read silently to p.5 and find the main character. Ask what people thought of this character's name. Talk about the character's response to people's reactions to her name.
- Write the words *deciduous* and *contagious* and have the children use dictionaries to check their meanings. Focus the children's attention on the letter patterns in these words, and list other words the children may know that end in *ous*.
- Turn to p.6. Ask the children to read silently and locate the name of the narrator. Draw the children's attention to the use of enlarged type for emphasis. Discuss other devices used for emphasis like bold type, italics, dashes and exclamation marks.

Reading

- Ask the children to read silently to the end of Chapter 3 after setting the focus questions:

  'What did Lucy's Mum do to help Lucy and Tree?'

  'How did Lucy feel about her mother's action?'

Early finishers can find examples of unusual type or punctuation in this section.

Discussing and examining the text

- First share the children's responses to the focus questions and then discuss the following:

  'What do you think will happen next? Why?'

- Throughout this section, there are many examples of enlarged type or unusual punctuation.
- Dashes are used on pp.8–9. Show how dashes are used to connect two parts of a sentence (one part is often an afterthought) or to add extra information.
- The ellipsis is used on p.6. Draw the children's attention to this and discuss its purpose.

Blackline Master 1 may be completed now.

Text Features and Teaching Opportunities

Use of the ellipsis
Use of enlarged type and italics for emphasis
Use of dashes
Vocabulary — words ending in ous
Format — letter
Abbreviations
Dictionary work

Synopsis

Tree tells Lucy that her family is moving away, and they decide to write letters. Lucy writes about her brother Brady, and how he is missing Tree's cat, Oatmeal. Tree writes about Oatmeal's strange behaviour and Lucy suggests that Oatmeal might be homesick. Then Oatmeal goes missing. Brady goes missing too, but is found curled up at a local store, with the owner's cat. Later, Oatmeal is found in Tree's old neighbourhood, playing with Brady. Tree lets Brady keep Oatmeal. Oatmeal has five kittens. When Lucy goes to visit Tree in the holidays, she gives her one of the kittens.

Session Two: Chapters 4, 5, and 6

Before reading

- Recall the content of the previous chapters.
- Encourage the children to review and alter their original predictions about the story.
- Read aloud pp.13–14 while the children track the text. Discuss the meaning and purpose of the abbreviation *P.T.O.* Discuss how this abbreviation has been formed.

Reading

- Direct the children to read independently to the end of Chapter 6 after setting the focus question:

  'What sorts of things are happening to Lucy and Tree?'

Early finishers may discuss or write what they think is wrong with Oatmeal.

Discussing and examining the text

- First share the children's responses to the focus question and then discuss the following:

  'What do you notice about the way the girls end their letters?'

  'How do the girls feel about being separated?'

  'What do you think is going to happen next in the story?'

Draw the children's attention to the unusual written conventions the children use in their letters.

Independent Reading

Have the children read the rest of the book independently after setting the focus questions:

'How have Lucy, Tree and Oatmeal changed since the beginning of the story?'

'Why do you think the author chose this title for the story?'

Blackline Master 2 (and **Blackline Master 1** if not done earlier) may be completed now.
Computer Task Centre Activity Card 11 may also be used now.

Emerald: Level 26

The Junkyard Dog

Wendy Macdonald

SESSION ONE: Chapters 1 and 2

Preparing for reading

- Look at the cover illustration and read the title. Ask the children to suggest what they would expect to see at a junkyard.
- Read the chapter titles on the contents page, then flick through the book and draw the children's attention to the illustrations. Ask them to predict what the story may be about.
- Turn to pp.4–5 and ask the children to read silently to find out what the dog is like. Discuss the concept of inferred meaning and talk about the difference between information that is *right there* on the page and the information that can be gained from reading *between the lines*. Ask them to reread the last paragraph and find the *between the lines* description of the dog.

Reading

- Direct the children to read silently to the end of Chapter 2 after setting the focus question:

  'Think about all the characters that have been introduced up to p.10, and work out what you have learnt about them.'

Early finishers can write about or discuss what they think of Stewart's actions.

Discussing and examining the text

- First share the children's responses to the focus question and then discuss the following:

  'What sort of information about the characters was *right there* on the page and what sort of information was *between the lines?*'

  'What do you think of Stewart's attitude and behaviour towards the dog?'

  'Why might Stewart be important in the story?'

- Ask the children to skim the text and find sentences that tell what happened in the past. Locate and list verbs written in the past tense and discuss how they are formed.

Blackline Master 1 may be completed now.

Text Features and Teaching Opportunities

First person recount — personal pronouns, past tense
Reading between the lines — inferred meaning
Direct and reported speech

Synopsis

Rachel meets a neglected dog in a junkyard and names him Prince. One day she sees Stewart tormenting Prince. She protests but Stewart doesn't care. When Prince is abandoned, Rachel takes him home. Later they meet Stewart and Rachel suggests that Stewart join the swimming club. He reluctantly begins training. A week before the swimming carnival, Rachel and Prince try to cross a flooded drain. Rachel is swept away by the water. Prince drags her out, and leads Stewart to Rachel. She misses the carnival but Stewart's team wins. Rachel realises that Prince saved her life.

SESSION TWO: Chapters 3 and 4

Before reading

- Recall the content of the previous chapters. Read the first paragraph on p.12 and ask the children to suggest what may have happened. Read the remaining text on the page to check children's predictions.

Reading

- Direct the children to read silently to the end of Chapter 4 after setting the focus questions:

  'In what ways does Prince change in these chapters?'

  'Find examples of Rachel's actions towards Stewart. Why did she act in these ways?'

Early finishers may discuss or write their predictions for the rest of the story.

Discussing and examining the text

- First share the children's responses to the focus questions, then discuss the following:

  'In what ways is Stewart different from Rachel?'

  'What information did you find out about Stewart from reading *between the lines*?'

- Throughout this section there are many examples of direct speech. Talk about the difference between reported and direct speech. Reread the direct speech on p.22. Demonstrate how this can be made into reported speech. Compare the features of direct and reported speech. Locate other examples of direct speech that the children could change to reported speech.

INDEPENDENT READING

Have the children read the rest of the book independently after setting the focus questions:

'Why wasn't Rachel concerned about not having won any races?'

'How would you describe each character?'

Blackline Master 2 (and **Blackline Master 1** if not done earlier) may be completed.
Computer Task Centre Activity Card 12 may also be used now.

Emerald: Level 26

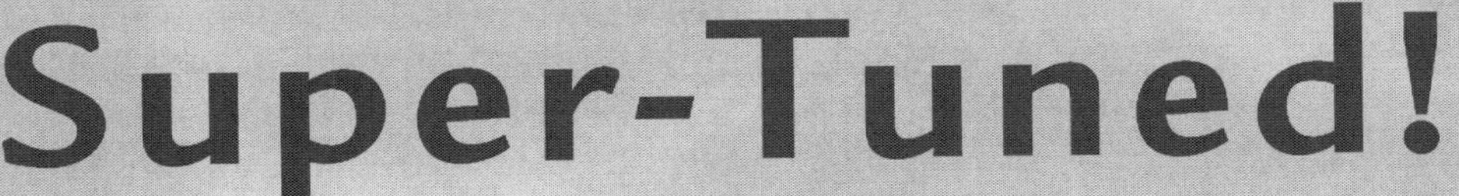

Super-Tuned!

Heather Hammonds

SESSION ONE: Chapters 1 and 2

Preparing for reading

- Look at the cover and read the title. Discuss possible meanings of the word *super-tuned*. Read the contents page, and ask the children to predict what the story might be about.
- Talk about hearing disability and encourage the children to share their knowledge.
- Draw the children's attention to the use of the hyphen in the word *super-tuned,* and discuss its purpose. List other words the children may know that have hyphens.
- Ask the children to read silently pp.4–5, then locate parts of the text that describe how Nick felt about his hearing aid.
- Draw the children's attention to the word *grumbled* as an alternative to *said.* Make a chart on which to record words that are used instead of *said.*

Reading

- Ask the children to read silently to p.11 after setting the focus questions:

  'How do Nick's feelings about his hearing aid change?'

  'What has made him feel this way?'

Early finishers can find words other than *said* to add to the chart.

Discussing and examining the text

- First share the children's responses to the focus questions and then discuss the following:

  'Why might the author have chosen the title *Super-Tuned*?'

  'What sort of fun could Nick have with his super-tuned hearing aid?'

  'Which other words has the author used instead of *said?*' (Add these words to the class chart.)

- Hyphenated words are used on p.7. Discuss the purpose of the hyphen.

Blackline Master 1 may be completed now.

Text Features and Teaching Opportunities

Third person narrative
Use of the hyphen
Vocabulary — words instead of said
Cause and effect
Conjunctions
Use of exclamation marks for emphasis
Direct speech
Apostrophe for contractions

Synopsis

Nick is worried that he will be teased about his new hearing aid. Nick and Adrian are in Nick's treehouse, when Nick hears music coming from the hearing aid. It seems to be tuning in to different radio frequencies. When Nick hears a distress signal from a fishing boat, the police drive Nick, his mum and Adrian to the Coastguard headquarters. Nick directs a helicopter pilot towards the source of the signal, and they find the boat. The rescued fishermen send him a stereo system as a 'thank you'. Nick decides that the hearing aid really is a good thing.

Session Two: Chapters 3 and 4

Before reading

- Recall the content of the previous chapters.
- Ask the children to silently read pp.12–13 and find out why Nick needed a hearing aid. Read the sentence that explains this, and observe the use of *because* to join *cause* and *effect*.

Reading

- Have the children read independently to the end of Chapter 4 after setting focus questions:

  'What does Nick hear that causes him to be very worried?'

  'What does he do?'

Discussing and examining the text

- First share the children's responses to the focus questions and then discuss the following:

  'Why would Nick feel so responsible for the fishermen?'

  'How would you feel if you were in his situation?'

- Throughout this section, there are many examples of words used to join sentences or parts of sentences. Ask the children to locate examples of words used to join sentences and introduce the term *conjunction*.
- Throughout this section, there are many examples of the use of exclamation marks for emphasis. Have the children skim the text to locate examples of this.

Independent Reading

Have the children read the rest of the book independently after setting the focus questions:

'What kinds of things did Nick have to do to help the police?'

'What do you think of his reward? Was it a good choice? Why?'

Blackline Master 2 (and **Blackline Master 1** if not done earlier) may be completed.
Computer Task Centre Activity Card 13 may also be used now.

Emerald: Level 26

The Crystal Unicorn

Julie Mitchell

Session One: Chapters 1 and 2

Preparing for reading

- Look at the cover illustration and read the title. Flick through the book and predict what the story may be about after looking at the chapter titles on the contents page.
- Ask the children to read pp.4–5 silently. Ask them to identify the name of the person telling the story and what the narrator felt about the crystal unicorn.
- Discuss how this story is written in the first person and explain the features of a text written in first person (use of personal pronouns *I, we, my, me, us, our* etc.).
- Discuss and list what the children know about unicorns. Discuss the prefix *uni* (meaning *one*), and brainstorm related words. Discuss the meaning of *crystal*.

Reading

- Direct the children to read silently to the end of Chapter 2 after setting the focus question:

  'What kind of girl is Gina and which actions make you think this?'

Early finishers can discuss or write who they predict may be outside Gina's door and their reasons for their predictions. They may use the dictionary to locate other words that begin with *uni*.

Discussing and examining the text

- First share the children's responses to the focus question, then discuss the following:

  'When did Gina first realise that what she had done was wrong?'

  'Why do you think Gina's mother didn't say something straight away when she found the crystal unicorn in Gina's room?'

Blackline Master 1 may be completed now.

Text Features and Teaching Opportunities

First Person narrative — personal pronouns
Vocabulary — meaning of uni
Use of speech marks in dialogue
Cause and effect
Dictionary work

Synopsis

While shopping with her mum, Gina sees a beautiful glass unicorn, and slips it into her pocket. But then she realises that she will never be able to enjoy it, because she stole it. She confesses to her mother, who had already found the unicorn in Gina's pocket. Gina returns the unicorn to the shop. She promises never to steal again. Mum suggests that Gina should do odd jobs to earn the money to buy the unicorn. When Gina makes the final payment on the unicorn, she puts it on her dressing table for everyone to enjoy.

SESSION TWO: Chapters 3 and 4

Before reading

- Recall the content of the previous chapters.
- Read the first sentence on p.13 and discuss the use of punctuation marks in direct speech. Ask the children to predict what Gina and her mother might say in this chapter. Write some examples on a class chart, noting the use of punctuation marks.

Reading

- Direct the children to read silently to the end of Chapter 4 after setting the focus questions:

  'What did Gina say to her mother and what were her mother's responses?'

  'What do you think of Gina's and her mother's actions?'

Early finishers may practise reading examples of direct speech using expression.

Discussing and examining the text

- First share the children's responses to the focus questions.

  'What are the effects of shoplifting as explained by the shopkeeper?'

- Throughout this section there have been many examples of cause and effect or action and consequence. Reread the last sentence on p.13 and locate in the text why Gina would never be able to enjoy the crystal unicorn. Discuss the use of *because* to join the cause and effect. Locate other sentences that include cause and effect or actions and consequence. Identify the words used to link these.

INDEPENDENT READING

Have the children read the rest of the book independently after setting the focus question:

'What did you learn as a result of reading this book?'

Blackline Master 2 (and **Blackline Master 1** if not done earlier) may be completed.
Computer Task Centre Activity Card 14 may also be used now.

Emerald: Level 26

Alfred the Curious

Jenny Hellen

Session One: Chapters 1 and 2

Preparing for reading

- Look at the cover illustration and read the title.
- Flick through Chapters 1 and 2 and draw the children's attention to the illustrations. Ask the children to predict when and where the story might be set, and what it might be about. Talk about the pictures and, where appropriate, use and clarify the meaning of words such as *spiral staircase, parapet, lances, pikes, archers, pages, knight, winches, lords, drawbridge*.
- Read aloud pp.4–5 while the children track the text. Ask them to retell in their own words what this part of the story is about.

Reading

- Ask the children to read silently to p.16 after setting the focus questions:

  'Who is preparing for battle and how are they doing this?'

  'What is Alfred doing during the preparations?'

Early finishers can discuss, list or draw who is preparing for battle.

Discussing and examining the text

- Share the children's responses to the focus questions.
- Throughout this section there are many examples of *auxiliary verbs*. Direct the children's attention to the actions of the characters, and discuss the use of extra words to create different forms of verbs. List examples of these 'helper verbs' and introduce the children to the term *auxiliary verbs*.
- Ellipses are used on p.12. Draw the children's attention to these and discuss their purpose.

Blackline Master 1 may be completed now.

Text Features and Teaching Opportunities

Third person narrative
Vocabulary — specialised vocabulary
Auxiliary verbs
Use of the ellipsis
Use of adjectives and verbs to enrich text
Vocabulary — onomatopoeic words
Cause and effect

Synopsis

Alfred sees Lord Edward's army riding towards the castle, pursued by Lord William's army. The battle for the castle begins. Lord Edward tells Alfred to go with Bartholomew to get some arrows from the storeroom. Here, Alfred hears Lord William's men tunnelling into the castle! Then Alfred sees that the tunnellers are using a hut at the base of the castle wall for protection. Lord Edward's men attack the tunnellers and Lord William's army retreats. Alfred's curiosity has helped save the day. He dreams of the day that he will ride his own horse into battle.

SESSION TWO: Chapters 3 and 4

Before reading

- Recall previous chapters. Ask the children to predict what will happen next.
- Direct the children to read silently p.17 and predict what the noise might be.
- Read aloud p.18. Ask the children to identify words used instead of *said*.
- Throughout this section there are many examples of *onomatopoeia*. Explain how onomatopoeic words sound like the action they describe. Ask the children to find examples of onomatopoeic words, such as *whizzing* on p.23.
- Ask the children to find the word on p.18 that describes the sound Alfred heard. Talk about the importance of writers using powerful adjectives and verbs to enrich the text.

Reading

- Direct the children to read silently to the end of Chapter 4 after setting the focus questions:

  'What was the noise and what are Bartholomew and Alfred afraid of?'

  'What do they plan to do?'

Early finishers may find the parts that describe what Bartholomew and Alfred are afraid of.

Discussing and examining the text

- First share the children's responses to the focus questions and then discuss the following:

  'What do you predict Lord Edward will do?'
- Turn to p.20, and ask the children to find what Alfred thought the enemy might do.
- Talk about cause and effect, and how the author has sequenced the actions.

INDEPENDENT READING

Have the children read the rest of the book independently after setting the focus questions:

'What qualities did Lord Edward think Alfred possessed?'

'Do you think Alfred really was curious? Find examples from the text to support your opinion.'

Blackline Master 2 (and **Blackline Master 1** if not done earlier) may be completed.
Computer Task Centre Activity Card 15 may also be used now.

Emerald: Level 25

Cathy Hope

Session One: Chapters 1–3

Preparing for reading

- Read the title and ask the children to suggest what sort of information they would expect to find in a book about yo-yos, and how this information might be grouped.
- Turn to the contents page. Ask the children what information they know that could be found in each chapter. Record this information on charts under chapter headings.
- Skim through the pages and note the visual features used to enhance the text.

Reading

- Direct the children to read silently to the end of p.13 after setting the focus questions:

  'Which countries have been associated with yo-yos?'

  'What materials have been used to make yo-yos?'

  'What have been the many uses of yo-yos over time?'

Early finishers can list all the different names used to refer to yo-yos.

Discussing and examining the text

- First share the children's responses to the focus questions and then discuss the following:

  'Yo-yos had many uses over time — what headings could be used to classify their uses?'

  'Yo-yos were made from a variety of materials. What are the advantages of plastic yo-yos compared with wooden ones?'
- Throughout this section, inverted commas or italics are used to indicate the different names given to yo-yos. Discuss the purpose of the inverted commas and italics.
- Use an atlas to locate the different countries mentioned in the text.

Blackline Master 1 may be completed now.

Text Features and Teaching Opportunities

Factual and procedural text
Vocabulary — specialised vocabulary
Use of visual text to enhance meaning — photographs, designs, illustrations
Use of inverted commas or italics to indicate alternative names
Dictionary work
Headings, Glossary and index

Synopsis

The yo-yo is the second-oldest known toy in the world and can be traced back through many centuries to Ancient Greece, Europe, Alaska and more recently, the Philippines and North America. A yo-yo depends on balance, weight, precision and gravity in order to perform well. Over the years, yo-yos have been made from a variety of materials, including wood and plastic. Children can make their own yo-yos and practise basic yo-yo skills by following step-by-step instructions. They can also learn tricks such as 'the spinner', 'walk the dog', 'around the world' and 'rock the baby'.

Session Two: Chapters 4–6

Before reading

- Recall the content of the previous chapters.
- Ask the children how yo-yos work, what parts make up a yo-yo and how yo-yos are made.

Reading

- Read aloud the first paragraph on p.14. Ask the children to identify any words whose meaning they are unsure of. Encourage them to use the glossary to work out the meanings. Then reread the paragraph, referring to the meanings from the glossary.
- Have the children silently read the rest of the page, using the glossary to assist them.
- Direct the children to read silently to the end of p.21 after setting the focus questions:

  'What materials can you use to make your own yo-yo?'

  'How can you make a yo-yo work better?'
- Early finishers can draw a flow chart of the production of a wooden or plastic yo-yo.

Discussing and examining the text

- Share the children's responses to the focus question and then discuss the following:

  'How has the author helped readers understand how yo-yos are made?'

  'What questions do you still have about the making of yo-yos?'
- Throughout this section, there are many examples of subject-specific information and terms. Ask the children to locate information by scanning the pages. (For example, turn to pp.12–13 and find names and purposes of tools used to make yo-yos. On p.13 find names for parts of yo-yos. On p.15 find materials that could be used for axles when making your own yo-yos.)

Independent Reading

Have the children independently read the rest of the book after setting the focus question:

'How does the author help you understand how to do the tricks?'

Blackline Master 2 (and **Blackline Master 1** if not done earlier) may be completed.
Computer Task Centre Activity Card 16 may also be used now.

Emerald: Level 25

The Pushcart Team

Amy Keystone as told to David Keystone

SESSION ONE: Pages 4–10 inclusive

Preparing for reading

- Read the title and ask the children to suggest another name for a pushcart, the steps needed to construct a pushcart, and the kinds of materials that could be used. Encourage discussion about the children's experiences with pushcarts.
- Skim through the pages noting the page layout as well as printed and visual text features. Talk about the purpose, structure and features of journal or diary entries.

Reading

- Direct the children to read silently to the end of p.11 after setting the focus questions:

  'Who are the people involved in the construction of the pushcart?'

  'How has each one become involved?'

  'What skills or help does each person offer?'

Early finishers can list the different characters and add information about them.

Discussing and examining the text

- First share the children's responses to the focus questions and then discuss the following:

  'In what ways is the information on pp.4–5 different from the other pages?'

  'How are the illustrations used to show information?'

- Draw the children's attention to the need to set the scene for the diary.
- Focus on the use of diagrams and the perspective. Introduce the term *bird's eye view*.
- Throughout this section there are examples of both direct and reported speech. Discuss the features of each kind of speech.

Blackline Master 1 may be completed now.

Text Features and Teaching Opportunities

First person recount — past tense
Factual and procedural text
Format — diary
Direct and reported speech
Vocabulary — specialised vocabulary
Use of visual text to enhance meaning — photographs, designs, illustrations
Labels and lists
Headings

Synopsis

Amy, Tina, Mansor and Ming-En ask Amy's father for advice about building a pushcart. They decide on a design and discuss the structure of the pushcart with Amy's dad. They collect all the materials, parts and tools that they will need, and start the building process. Soon, the job is finished, but they still haven't found a name for the pushcart. They make a list of safety gear that will be needed for training. The team meets to practise and watch some of the other teams. They finally make a decision about the name of the pushcart — Team Spirit.

SESSION TWO: Pages 1–20 inclusive

Preparing for reading

- Recall the content of the previous chapters.
- Ask the children to suggest the different parts of a pushcart. Compile a class list. Turn to p.13 and look at the parts of the pushcart. Compare this to the children's suggestions.

Reading

- Direct the children to read silently to the end of p.20 after setting the focus questions:
  'What safety gear and tools do they need to complete the pushcart?'
  'Three places were suggested for practice sessions with the pushcart. Where were these places and why was each suggested?'

Early finishers can list or share the questions they would ask about building a pushcart.

Discussing and examining the text

- Share the children's responses to the focus questions and then discuss the following:
  'How has the author provided factual information? Why is it presented in this way?'
  'What questions would you ask Dad and Mrs Walipoor about building a pushcart?'
  'Why would they have suggested the names listed on p.16?'
- Throughout this section, there are many examples of subject-specific information. Ask the children to locate specific information by scanning the text. (For example, turn to p.11 and find out why ball bearings help the wheels turn smoothly, or p.12 to find out what will be placed in the drilled holes. Turn to p.14 to find out who put the wheels on, and turn to p.15 to find out who suggested a practice session at Greenmount Lake.)

INDEPENDENT READING

Have the children read the rest of the book independently after setting the focus question:
'What do the children call the pushcart?'

Blackline Master 2 (and **Blackline Master 1** if not completed earlier) may be completed now.
Computer Task Centre Activity Card 17 may also be used now.

Emerald: Level 25

Snowboarding Diary

June Stratford and Jane Morrison

SESSION ONE: Day 1 and 2

Preparing for reading

- Read the title and ask the children to brainstorm what they know about snowboarding. Make a chart and list the information under headings; for example, *skills required, clothing, equipment, places, special terms*. List any questions that may arise from the brainstorming.

Reading

- Ask the children to read silently to the end of Day 2 after setting the focus questions:

  'If you were to prepare for a snowboarding trip, what things would you need and what things would you do?'

  'What information do the illustrations provide about snowboarding?'

- Early finishers can select an item of clothing or equipment and list all the details they can find about it in the text.

Discussing and examining the text

- First share the children's responses to the focus questions and then discuss the following:

  'Why do you think the authors chose to have one of the characters come from Jamaica?'

  'What was the purpose of the first chapter of this book?'

- Draw the children's attention to the structure of the text. Discuss the use of the first person narrative and how the text is presented as a recount of events. Focus on the use of the past tense to retell the story, but draw the children's attention to the use of the present tense to describe people and events on p.5 and p.7. Ask the children to check whether the authors give the name of the reteller in the first chapter.

Blackline Master 1 may be completed now.

Text Features and Teaching Opportunities

Vocabulary — specialised vocabulary
First person recount — past and present tense
Factual text
Compound words
Use of the hyphen
Use of visual text to enhance meaning — inserts, diagrams, photographs, illustrations
Glossary and index
Cause and effect

Synopsis

Jasmine has come from Jamaica to go snowboarding with Jane. Can they adapt their skateboarding skills to snowboarding? When they reach the snowfields, they learn that there will be a snowboarding competition for beginners. The instructor gives the girls a list of safety rules. They go up the mountain on a chairlift with their snowboarding class, but they have an accident on the slopes and the ski patrol takes them back to the lodge. Later, they practise and head off to the competition on the chairlift. Jasmine finishes without a fall, but Jane crashes out. Jasmine comes second.

SESSION TWO: Days 3 and 4

Before reading

- Recall the content of the previous chapters.
- Conduct a 'Possible Sentences' activity that sets a context and focus for their reading. (For further details on this teaching procedure, see Jennings, C. & Shephard, J. 1998, *Literacy and the Key Learning Areas,* Eleanor Curtain Publishing, Armadale). List the following words: *bindings, toe turns, heel turns, loading station, leash*. Ask the children to write sentences about snowboarding using these words.

Reading

- Direct the children to read silently to the end of Day 4 after setting the focus questions:

  'What are the main safety rules for snowboarding?'

  'What do toe and heel turns help snowboarders to do?'

Early finishers can check their sentences from the 'Possible Sentences' activity against the information they have gained from their reading.

Discussing and examining the text

- Compare the children's original sentences from the 'Possible Sentences' activity with what they have learnt from the text. Share responses to the focus questions, then discuss:

  'How have the authors provided the factual information?'

- Draw the children's attention to the way in which general factual information about snowboarding is combined with specific information about the reteller's own experiences. Help the children to locate examples of general factual information.

INDEPENDENT READING

Have the children read the rest of the book independently after setting the focus question:

'What have you learnt about snowboarding from reading this book'?

Blackline Master 2 (and **Blackline Master 1** if not done earlier) may be completed.
Computer Task Centre Activity Card 18 may also be used now.

Emerald: Level 26

Skateboarding

Serena Ramsay

SESSION ONE: Chapters 1 and 2

Preparing for reading

- Encourage the children to discuss what they know about skateboards. Draw a concept map with different facts about skateboards. Encourage the children to provide links between each fact.

Reading

- Direct the children to read silently to the end of Chapter 2 after setting the focus questions:

  'What would you need to think about when buying a skateboard?'

  'What did the author need to know to be able to write Chapter 2?

- Early finishers can list any questions they can think of about the information in Chapter 1, and some of the facts provided in Chapter 2.

Discussing and examining the text

- First share the children's responses to the focus questions. Provide opportunities for the early finishers to share their questions with the class.
- Discuss the following:

  'How can riders check that their skateboards are suitable for them'?

  'What do you think about having to purchase special clothing to wear?'

- Organise a skateboard day during which the children can share their skateboarding skills and any further research they have done on skateboards.

Blackline Master 1 may be completed now.

Text Features and Teaching Opportunities

Third person narrative — past and present tense
Instructional and persuasive text
Format — letters and reports
Visual features to enhance meaning — diagrams
Dictionary work
Compound words
Glossary and index

Synopsis

Todd buys a skateboard and learns about its parts. He buys safety gear and reads about the history of skateboarding in a magazine. Todd and his friends skateboard outside the local library. But an article in the local newspaper warns that skateboarders will be fined if they skate there. Todd writes to the newspaper, saying that there is nowhere else for skateboarders to go. The librarian argues that skateboarders make it hard for people to use the library. Todd organises a petition, asking the council to provide a skatepark. A few months later a new skatepark is built.

Session Two: Chapters 3 and 4

Before reading

- Recall the content of the previous chapters.
- Read aloud the next two chapter titles and ask the children to predict what they think the chapters might be about.

Reading

- Have the children read silently to the end of Chapter 4 after setting focus questions:
  'What is the important information about the development of the skateboard?'
  'How did the author choose to present this information? Why?'
  'What steps must new skateboarders take to develop their skills?'

Early finishers can draw a timeline of the development of the skateboard.

Discussing and examining the text

- Share responses to the focus questions. Then discuss the following:
  'What do the terms 'goofy foot' and 'regular foot' mean?'
- Draw the children's attention to the meanings presented in the glossary.
- Show how instructions are written in present tense. Note how visual features enhance the text. Focus on the use of verbs in instructions. Ask the children to find the verbs.

Independent Reading

Have the children independently read the rest of the book after setting the focus questions:
'What are some of the problems involved with skateboarding?'
'From whose point of view are these problems presented?'

Revisit the concept map from Session One and encourage the children to suggest alterations based on the information they have learnt from reading the book.

Blackline Master 2 (and **Blackline Master 1** if not done earlier) may be completed.
Computer Task Centre Activity Card 19 may also be used now.

Emerald: Level 26

Kites

Cheryl Jakab

Session One: Chapters 1 and 2

Preparing for reading

- Read aloud the title and chapter headings while the children track the text. Flick through Chapters 1 and 2 and draw the children's attention to the page layout and use of visual text.
- Make a chart listing each question from p.5 on separate large sheets of paper. Ask the children to discuss and add what they know under each question.

Reading

- Have the children silently read to the end of Chapter 2 after setting a focus question:

  'What can you find out about the history of kites?'
- Early finishers can skim through the pages and write all the key words relating to people and places associated with kites.

Discussing and examining the text

- First share the children's responses to the focus question and then discuss the following:

  'What have been some of the uses of kites?'

  'Why do you think China is considered the home of the kite?'

  'How would kites have helped people from the South Seas with their fishing?'
- Draw the children's attention to the title of the second chapter. Discuss why the author may have used this title. Talk about how authors use language in many different ways. For example, words that sound the same but are spelt differently or have different meanings are called *homophones*. Discuss and list examples of homophones and encourage the children to suggest other words or phrases that they know which may have two meanings.
- Revisit the questions on the charts and ask the children to add any other information that they have gained from reading.

Blackline Master 1 may be completed now.

Text Features and Teaching Opportunities

Factual and procedural text
Vocabulary — specialised vocabulary
Use of homophones
Diagrams and labels
Vocabulary — the meaning of aero
Headings
Glossary and index
Dictionary work

Synopsis

Kite-flying is fun, and many kite festivals are held all around the world to celebrate the wonder of the kite. Kites have a long history in Asia and the Pacific. Kites have performed important roles in the history of technology. Information includes the different parts of a kite, the aerodynamics of a kite and how to fly a kite in a variety of conditions, as well as safety rules. Children can make a simple diamond kite by following the step-by-step instructions and learn about the variety of modern kites available today.

SESSION TWO: Chapters 3 and 4

Before reading

- Recall the content of the previous chapters.
- Encourage the children to ask questions about what they have read so far.
- Ask the children to describe the features of a basic kite shape.

Reading

- Direct the children to read silently to the end of Chapter 4 after setting focus questions:
  'What are the main parts of the kite and what are their functions?'
  'What is meant by the *aerodynamics* of the kite?'
  'What would you tell people if they are about to fly a kite for the first time?'

Early finishers can write questions about the content in Chapter 4.

Discussing and examining the text

- First share the children's responses to the focus question and ask early finishers to present some of their questions to the class. Discuss the following:
  'What are the main things a kite needs to fly properly?'
  'How does the placement of the tether affect the flight of the kite?'
  'Why would it be dangerous to fly a kite in a thunderstorm?'
- Ask the children to suggest labels for the parts of a kite, and make a class chart.
- Discuss the meaning of the word *aerodynamics*. List words with the prefix *aero*.
- Revisit the question charts from Session One and add any further information that the children have read under each question.

INDEPENDENT READING

Have the children independently read the rest of the book. Later, ask them to construct their own kite (refer to Chapter 5).

Organise a kite day for the children to share the kites they have made, and any further research that they have done on kites.

Blackline Master 2 (and **Blackline Master 1** if not done earlier) may be completed.
Computer Task Centre Activity Card 20 may also be used now.

Emerald: Level 26

The Bicycle Book

Anna Fern

Session One: Chapters 1, 2 and 3

Preparing for reading

- Read the title and ask the children to predict the type of book that this might be; for example, fiction or non-fiction (factual).
- Ask the children to suggest the kind of information they would expect to find in a factual book about bicycles. Make a list of broad categories and headings for information and discuss how this information may be organised and presented. Turn to the contents page and compare the chapter titles with the children's predictions.
- Draw the children's attention to the titles of the first three chapters and ask them to brainstorm everything that they know about bicycle parts, clothing and safety equipment.

Reading

- Direct the children to read silently to the end of Chapter 3 after setting the focus question:

  'If you were to become an expert in bicycle parts, clothing and safety equipment, what information would you get from these chapters?'

Early finishers can compare their predictions about what information may be in the book with the information that they actually find.

Discussing and examining the text

- First share the children's responses to the focus question and then discuss the following:

  'How did the author provide information about the bicycle parts?'

- Draw the children's attention to the use of labels and insets to add information to the text.
- Ask the children to skim pp.6–7 and find the reasons for wearing a helmet, bright clothing, cycling gloves and sunglasses.

Blackline Master 1 may be completed now.

Text Features and Teaching Opportunities

Factual and procedural text
Vocabulary — specialised vocabulary
Headings and subheadings
Labels
Cause and effect
Dictionary work
Use of brackets
Glossary and index

Synopsis

Before you start riding, you need to learn about your bike and how to ride it safely. Information includes the parts of a bike, standard fittings and extras, how to tell if the bike is the right size, and the right clothing for biking, focusing on safety and comfort. It is important to practise bike-riding skills and to know how to use brakes and gears before going out onto the road. You also need to learn the road rules, how to ride defensively, how to maintain a bike properly, how to fix a puncture, and what to do in an accident.

SESSION TWO: Chapters 4, 5 and 6

Preparing for reading

- Recall the content of the previous chapters.
- Conduct an anticipation activity that draws on the children's prior knowledge and sets a context and focus for their reading. List the following statements:
  'Pedalling is easier when you push with all of your foot.'
  'You have to be pedalling to change gears.'
  'Gears help you ride faster and use more energy.'
  'One of the common causes of bicycle accidents is cyclists failing to stop at intersections.'
  The children should consider each statement and write whether it is true or false.

Reading

- Direct the children to read silently to the end of Chapter 6, keeping both the statements from the anticipation activity and their responses in mind.
- Early finishers may form other statements to use in a true/false activity.

Discussing and examining the text

- First compare the children's responses in the anticipation activity with what they have learnt from the text. Then discuss the following:

  'Are there any words in the text that you have not seen before?'

Talk about the use of specialised or subject-specific vocabulary in factual reports.

- Throughout Chapter 5, headings and subheadings are used. Discuss how this helps the reader to locate different kinds of information.

INDEPENDENT READING

Direct the children, in pairs or small groups, to predict the steps in changing a flat tyre. Have the children read the rest of the book independently after setting the focus questions:

'What are the steps that you need to take to change a tyre?'

'What are the main road safety rules to remember when riding your bike?'

Blackline Master 2 (and **Blackline Master 1** if not done earlier) may be completed.
Computer Task Centre Activity Card 21 may also be used now.

Emerald: Level 26

Funny Business

An Anthology of Humour

SESSION ONE

Preparing for reading

- Read the title and look at the cover illustration. Read aloud the titles on the contents page. Then ask the children to predict what the book might be about.
- Introduce the term *anthology* and discuss what it means. Ask the children to skim through the pages to develop an awareness of the structure and features of this anthology. Compile a chart to record the children's knowledge about anthologies.
- The following sessions show how the anthology could be used. They suit small group work because they focus children's attention on specific reading skills and knowledge.

SESSION TWO: *Woof*

Synopsis

Ten-year-old Eric is lying in bed when he realises that he is turning into a dog. How will he tell his friend Roy — and what will his little sister Emily and his parents think?

Before reading

- Read aloud the first sentence and ask the children to predict what might happen in the story.

Reading

- Ask them to read silently to the end of the story after setting the focus question:

  'What were all the personal qualities Eric possessed?'

Discussing and examining the text

- First share the children's responses to the focus question and then discuss the following:

  'Why do you think this story was included in the anthology?'

  'What did you think of the story? Why? What type of story is this?'
- Discuss the differences between realistic fiction and fantasy. Ask the children to discuss, draw or write what might happen to Eric now that he has changed into a dog.

Text Features and Teaching Opportunities

Purpose, structure and features of an anthology
Different text formats with related theme — first person narrative, third person narrative, fiction, explanatory text, informative text, descriptive text, poetry, lists
Use of italics for emphasis
Use of adjectives and verbs to enrich text
Use of open and closed questions
Use of personal pronouns
Literal meaning

SESSION THREE: *Reasons we can't get a dog*

Synopsis

A parent has an answer to every plea for the family to get a dog.

Before reading

- Read the title and ask the children to discuss their experiences with pet dogs. Make a class chart and list any reasons the children can think of for not getting a dog.

Reading

- Ask the children to read silently to the end of the story after setting the focus questions:

  'From whose point of view is this text written?'

  'Who do you think was listing the reasons why they couldn't get a dog?'

Discussing and examining the text

- First share the children's responses to the focus questions and then discuss the following:

  'To whom do you think the narrator is talking?'

  'What would be the responses to some of the narrator's comments?'

  'How do you know this?'

- Look at the 'gaps' in the text where the narrator has responded to a second person's comments or questions. The children can suggest what the missing dialogue could be.
- Revisit the class chart and list reasons in favour of getting a dog.

SESSION FOUR: *Digger reckons*

Synopsis

Life from a doggy point of view. Digger gets off-side with his young owner, tries to frighten the neighbour's cat and gives the elderly neighbour a good scare. Then Digger creates havoc in the house when he tries to evade the dog-catcher. And when Digger realises he isn't going to get the left-over scraps from his owners' dinner, he plans his next bit of mischief.

Before reading

- Revisit the children's experiences with pet dogs from Session Three. Ask the children to discuss what sort of antics their dogs get up to, what their dogs like doing, and why they think their dogs like behaving this way.

Reading

- Ask the children to read silently to the end of the story after setting the following focus questions:

  'Why do you think the author chose this title?'
  'From whose point of view is the story written?'

Discussing and examining the text

- First share the children's responses to the focus questions and then discuss the following:

  'How did the author indicate the main character's thoughts?'
  'If you had to describe Digger's nature what would you say? Why?'
  'If you were Digger's owner what would you do? Why?'

- Discuss the way italics can be used to present different kinds of information. Ask the children to skim through the pages of this story and note how italics are used.
- Draw the children's attention to the author's use of language to create vivid images. Ask them to locate action verbs and groups of words that refer to or describe the verbs.
- The children can discuss the actions of their own dogs or dogs they know. Ask them to write these actions in third person narrative and then use first person narrative to write about the actions from the dogs' point of view; for example, 'The dog chewed the bone. Oh, this is delicious!'

Blackline Master 1 may be completed now.

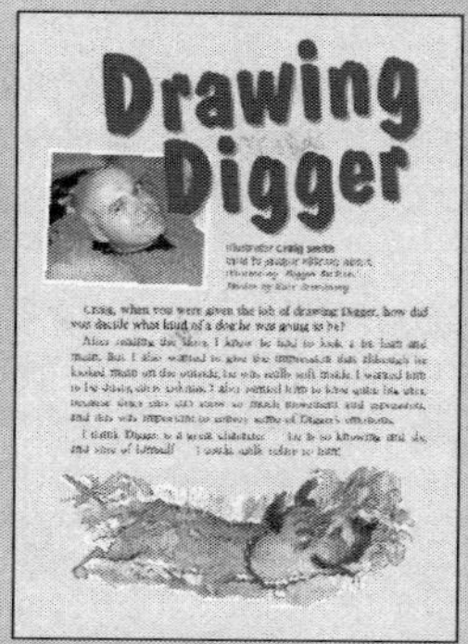

SESSION FIVE: *Drawing Digger*

Synopsis

Interview format of questions and answers with popular illustrator Craig Smith.

Before reading

- Compile a class list of any questions that the children would like to ask the illustrator, Craig Smith, about his illustrations for *Digger Reckons*.
- Talk about the use of open and closed questions. Ask the children which kind of questions will help gather more information.
- Read aloud the first question while the children track the text. Ask the children to silently read the answer for this question. Discuss what they found out. Then repeat this process with the next two questions.

Reading

- Ask the children to read silently to the end of the story after setting the focus question:

  'What have you learnt about the illustrator and the illustrations?'

Discussing and examining the text

- First share the children's responses to the focus question and then discuss the following:

  'What is the difference between laughing at and laughing with someone?'
- Revisit the class list of questions and check whether the information in the text provided the answers. If not, ask the children how they would find out the answers for the remaining questions.
- The children can research more books by Craig Smith, and use this information to create a biography about Craig Smith.

The school play

Session Six: *The school play*

Synopsis

Two brothers, Paddy and Fieldsy are in the school play. When their sister Lee tells them that all the great actors have butterflies in the stomach before a performance, Fieldsy has a novel way of ensuring that he gets butterflies.

Before reading

- Read the title and encourage the children to describe their experiences in school plays.

Reading

- Ask the children to read silently to the end of the story after setting the focus question:
  'What was the misunderstanding that led to the funny ending in this story?'

Discussing and examining the text

- First share the children's responses to the focus question and then discuss the following:
  'From whose point of view was the story written?'
  'Fieldsy misunderstood the actual meaning of the phrase *butterflies in your stomach*. What does it really mean?'
- Draw the children's attention to the use of first person narrative and ask them to locate the first person pronouns in this story.
- Draw the children's attention to the concept of literal meaning. Ask the children to suggest any sayings they may know, where the literal meaning is different from the meaning in everyday usage.
- Ask the children to talk or write about times they have been nervous and what helps them to overcome their nervousness.

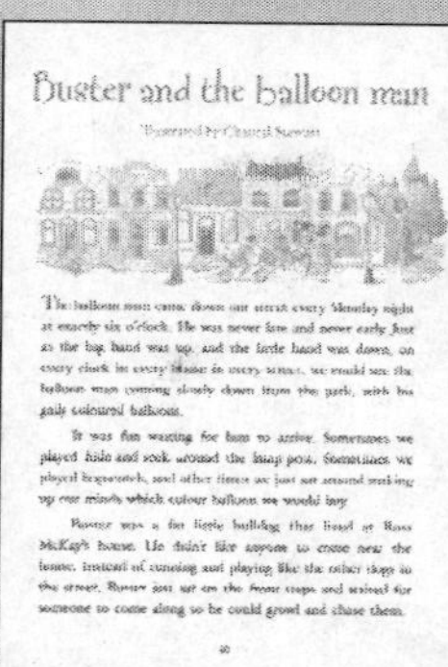

SESSION FOUR: *Buster and the balloon man*

Synopsis

Buster the bulldog doesn't like the balloon man who visits every Monday night. Buster torments the balloon man and forces him to run back up the street to the park where no dogs are allowed. One night the balloon man comes with special floating balloons instead of balloons on sticks. He attaches Buster to a big balloon and Buster floats away. When Buster comes back he is a changed dog.

Before reading

- Read the title. Summarise the story for the children. (A dog menaces a balloon-seller and prevents him from proceeding along a street to sell his balloons to the residents.)
- Ask the children to suggest different ways of stopping the dog from doing this.

Reading

- Ask the children to read silently to the end of the story after setting the focus question:

  'How was the problem resolved?'

Discussing and examining the text

First share the children's responses to the focus question and then discuss the following:

'From whose point of view was the story written?'

'How do you think Buster returned to the house?'

'How did Buster's behaviour change from the beginning to the end of the story?'

Discuss the way a responsible dog-owner should behave. Ask the children to suggest how Buster's owner could have changed his behaviour.

Independent reading

- Have the children independently read the rest of the anthology. When the reading is complete, ask the children to reflect on how they went about reading the anthology and the way in which it was different from reading a chapter book or story.

Blackline Master 2 (and **Blackline Master 1** if not done earlier) can be completed.
Computer Task Centre Activity Card 22 may also be used now.

SYNOPSES FOR THE REMAINING PIECES

10 things your parents will never say
A list of directives children would love to hear. Can be used with 'Tidying my room'.

The dangerous dinosaur
Rhyming verse about the most fearful characteristic of a dinosaur — its bad breath!

Funny business
Christine Powell has a business that has many funny moments: it's an acting agency for animals. Learn how animals are trained, about animals' 'make-up' and finding the right animal for a part. Read about a day in the life of Jet the cat actor, who has a part in a TV serial.

Magnetic madness
On a school excursion to the science museum, Tom Williams misbehaves because he has eaten too many fruit bars with lots of vitamins, minerals and sugar. Tom stands in front of the magnetic field generators when they are turned on and claims he is magnetised. Tom gets a lecture on his behaviour from his teacher, who is using a computer. When Tom stands near the computer it blows up. Perhaps he is magnetised. For the rest of the day Tom attracts metal objects. He visits his gran, who is a scientist. Gran comes up with a solution — a hot bath to de-magnetise Tom.

Fruit
The supermarket fruit and vegetables want a life of their own. They convince Tanya the trolley girl that they need some time out, and so she takes them to the beach. No wonder supermarket fruit and vegetables look a bit tired sometimes.

Tidying my room
Provides a quick solution to a perennial problem. Can be used with 'Ten things your parents will never say' and as a model for writing verse about similar topics.

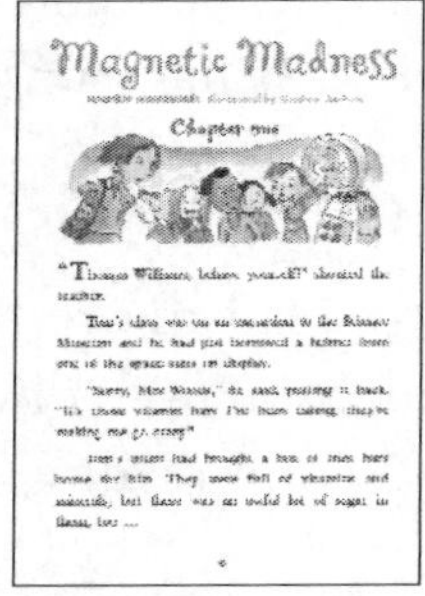

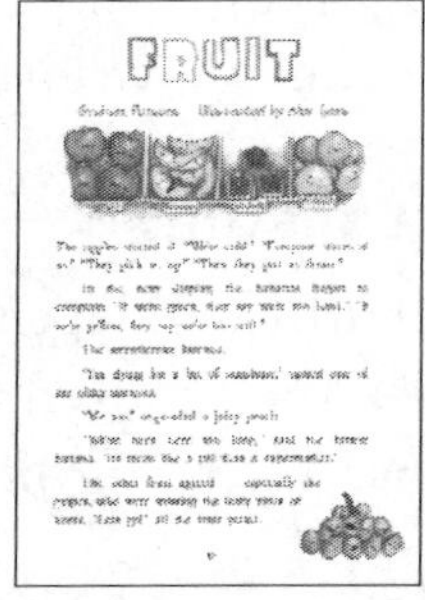

List of blackline masters

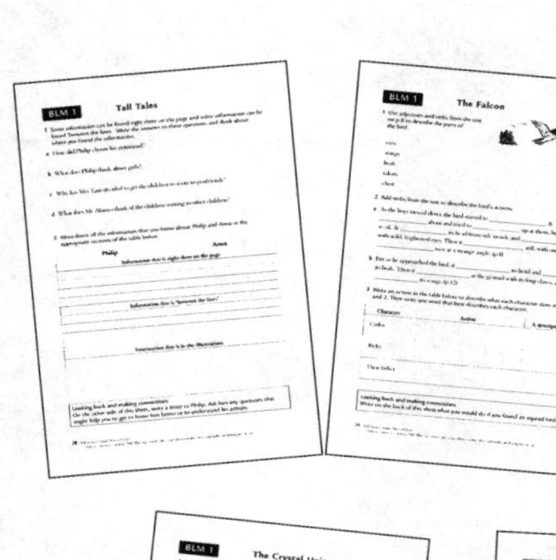
BLM 1 Tall Tales
BLM 1 The Falcon

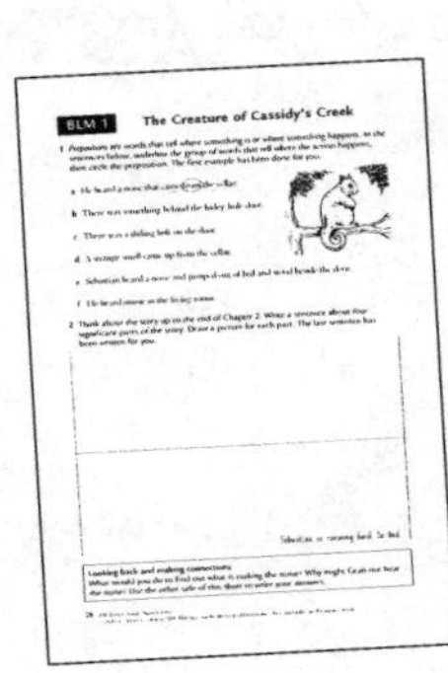
BLM 1 The Creature of Cassidy's Creek

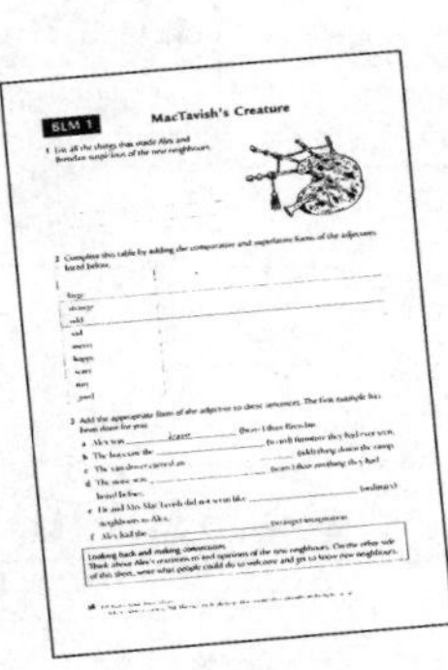
BLM 1 MacTavish's Creature

BLM 2 The Trouble with Oatmeal

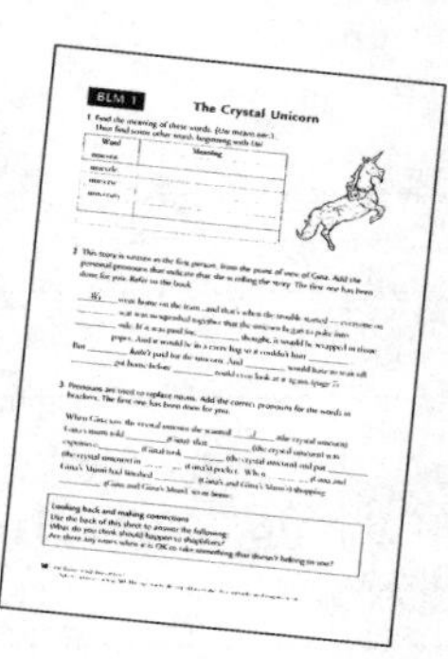
BLM 1 The Crystal Unicorn

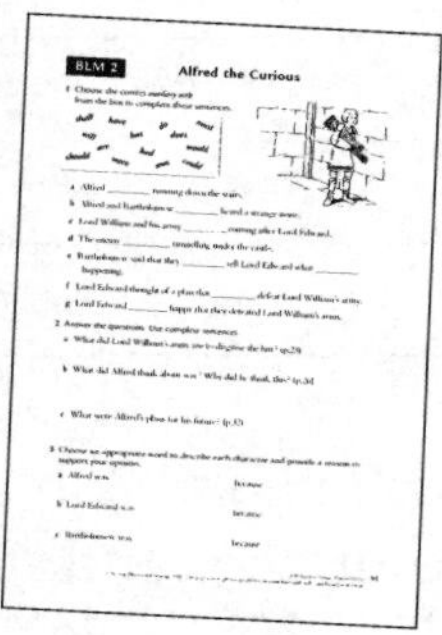
BLM 2 Alfred the Curious

BLM 2 Snowboarding Diary

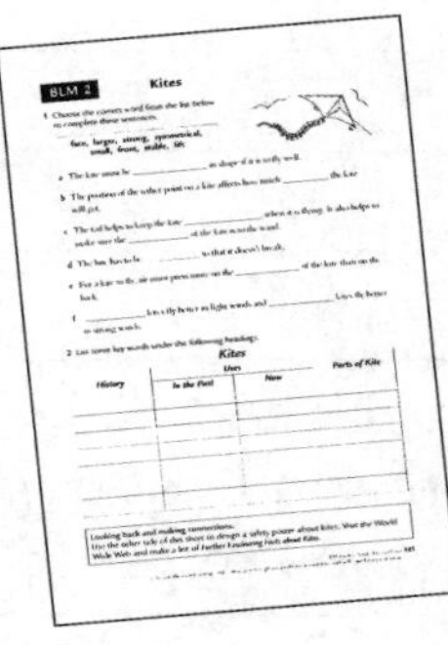
BLM 2 Kites

BLM 1 Tall Tales

1 Some information can be found right there on the page and other information can be found 'between the lines'. Write the answers to these questions and think about where you found the information.

a How did Philip choose his penfriend? ____________________

b What does Philip think about girls? ____________________

c Why has Mrs Tam decided to get the children to write to penfriends? ____________________

d What does Mr Alonzo think of the children writing to other children? ____________________

2 Write down all the information that you know about Philip and Anna in the appropriate sections of the table below.

Philip	Anna
Information that is right there on the page	
Information that is 'between the lines'	
Information that is in the illustrations	

Looking back and making connections
On the other side of this sheet, write a letter to Philip. Ask him any questions that might help you to get to know him better or to understand his actions.

BLM 2 Tall Tales

1 Write down the questions from the following pages of the text. Then colour the boxes to show whether they are open or closed questions. Write the answer for each question.

a (p.10) Question: ______________________

Answer: ______________________ | open | closed |

b (p.16) Question: ______________________

Answer: ______________________ | open | closed |

c (p.19) Question: ______________________

Answer: ______________________ | open | closed |

d (p.21) Question: ______________________

Answer: ______________________ | open | closed |

d (p.21) Question: ______________________

Answer: ______________________ | open | closed |

2 Choose words from the box that describe Philip. Then find an example from the story to show when he acted this way. The first example has been done for you.

surprised	worried	dishonest	slow	annoyed	embarrassed	sneaky

Philip

Annoyed	When he had to write to a girl
	______________________
	______________________
	______________________

BLM 1 The Secret

1 Chris Draper has many personal qualities. Write examples of Chris's actions that show he has the qualities listed in the table below.

Quality	Action
brave	
considerate	
proud	
athletic	

2 Words with the same meaning are called *synonyms*. Write words from the story that mean the same as the words listed below. Then use a dictionary or thesaurus to find another word with the same meaning.

Meaning	Word	Synonym
a guard (p.4)	__________	__________
b replacement (p.6)	__________	__________
c hurt (p.9)	__________	__________
d gasping (p.10)	__________	__________
e weary (p.12)	__________	__________

Looking back and making connections
On the other side of this sheet, write what you know about asthma.

BLM 2 The Secret

1 Andrew experienced many feelings and acted in different ways during the story. Complete each sentence below with an example from the text.

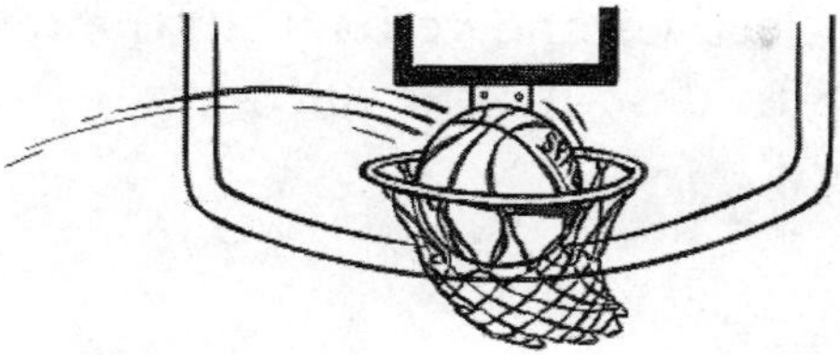

a Andrew panicked when ______________________________.

b Andrew was exhausted when ______________________________.

c Andrew was embarrassed when ______________________________.

d Andrew was trapped when ______________________________.

e Andrew was foolish when ______________________________.

f Andrew was surprised when ______________________________.

2 Pronouns are used to replace nouns. Circle all the pronouns in the box.

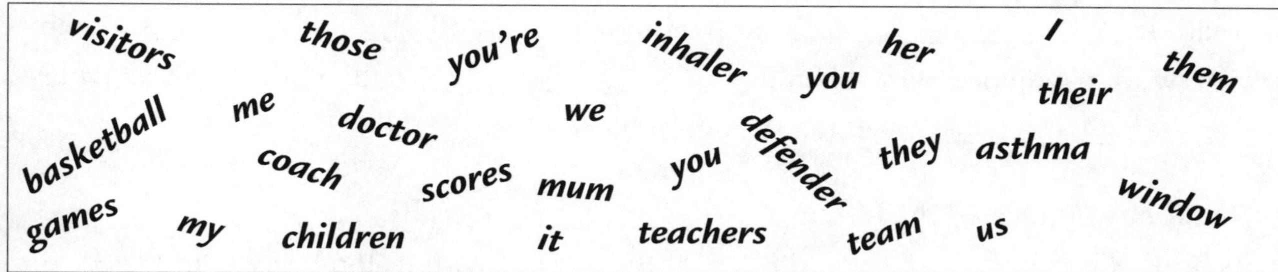

3 Write pronouns for the nouns in brackets to complete the sentences.

a Andrew had a puffer to use before ____________ (Andrew) played basketball.

b Andrew would not use ______________ (Andrew's) puffer in front of Chris because ____________ (Andrew) felt embarrassed.

c ______________ (Andrew's mum) visited ______________ (Andrew) in hospital.

d ________________(Chris and his mum) visited ______________ (Andrew) and ______________ (Chris) told ____________ (Andrew) about ________________ (Chris's) asthma.

e ______________ (asthma) affects ______________ (people's) breathing.

4 On the other side of this sheet, draw a story map to show the main parts of the story.

BLM 1 The Falcon

1 Use adjectives and verbs from the text on p.8 to describe the parts of the bird.

eyes ____________________

wings ____________________

beak ____________________

talons ____________________

chest ____________________

2 Add verbs from the text to describe the bird's actions.

a As the boys moved closer, the bird started to ____________. It ____________ about and tried to ____________ up at them, but it was too weak. It ____________ its head from side to side and ____________ at them with wild, frightened eyes. Then it ____________ still, with one of its wings ____________ over at a strange angle. (p.8)

b But as he approached the bird, it ____________ its head and ____________ its beak. Then it ____________ at the ground with its long claws, and tried to ____________ its wings. (p.12)

3 Write an action in the table below to describe what each character does in Chapters 1 and 2. Then write one word that best describes each character.

Character	Action	A descriptive word
Carlos		
Ricky		
Their father		

Looking back and making connections
Write on the back of this sheet what you would do if you found an injured bird.

BLM 2 The Falcon

Summarise the story in the right sequence to complete this flow chart of the story. Draw pictures for each part.

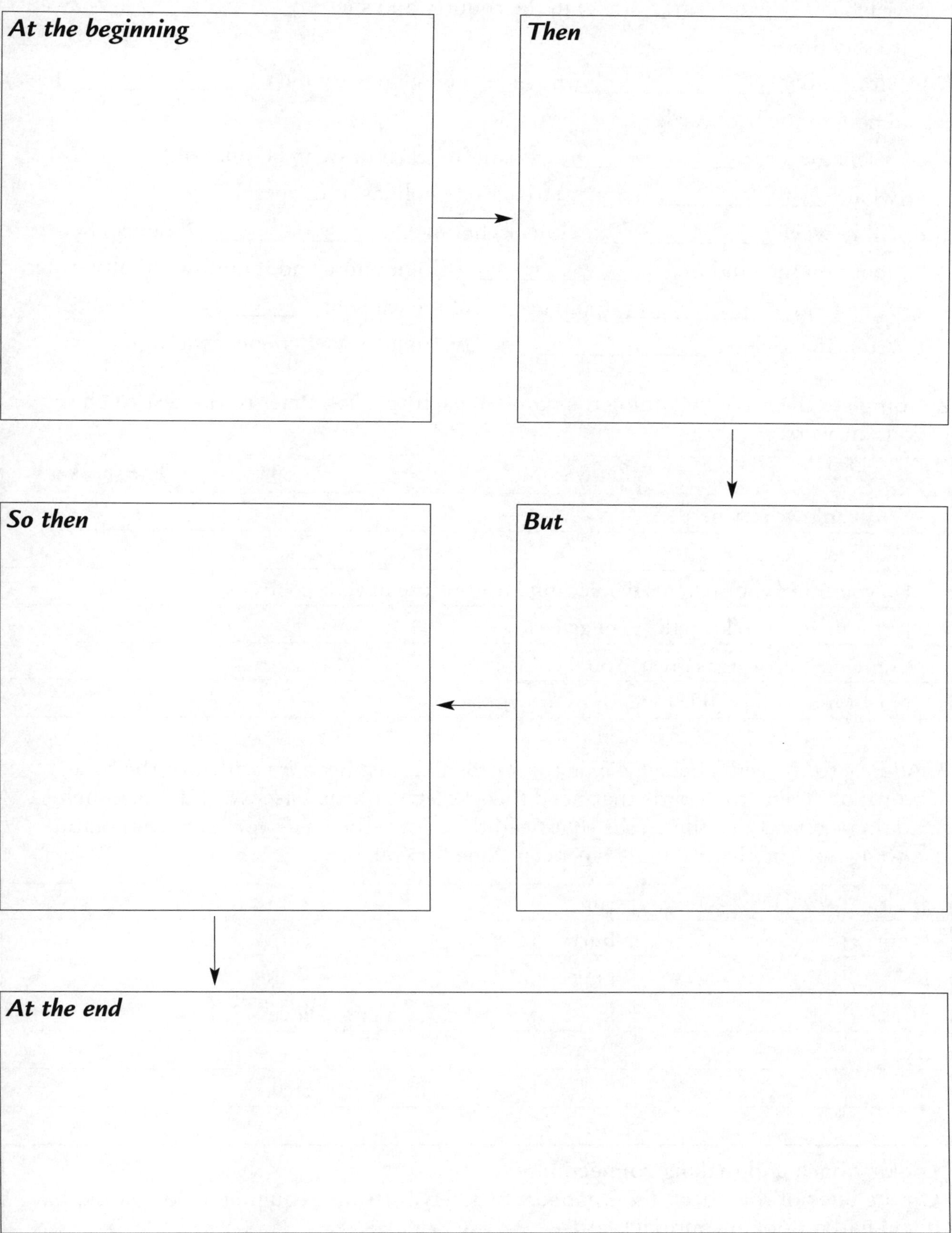

BLM 1 Queen of the Pool

1 Write the verbs in brackets in the past tense to complete these sentences.

a Selena ________________ (live) in the country and she ____________________ (want) to stay there.

b Her family ________________ (move) to a new house, which ________________(have) a pool in the backyard.

c Selena never _________________ (want) to learn to swim because of what________________ (happen) to her one holiday at the beach.

d A big wave ________________ (knock) her over, ________________ (bounce) her about on the sand and ________________ (fill) her nose and mouth with salty water.

e A woman ______________ (pull) her out of the water and ______________ (rescue) her.

f After that Selena ________________ (refuse) to go anywhere near the water.

2 Complete the table by adding the name of each speaker. Refer to the text to check your answers.

What was said	The speaker
"Why can't we stay here?"	
"She'll get over it."	
"Do you think your parents would mind if I practise in your pool?"	
"Just remember to keep the pool gate closed."	
"Come in. The water's great. You'll enjoy it."	
"Now Mum will be able to teach us to swim."	

3 Add *ing* to the verbs below. Circle the words that just need *ing* added to the base word; underline the words that need the last letter of the base word doubled before adding *ing*; and tick the words that need the *e* from the base word removed before adding *ing*. The first example has been done for you.

say	saying	run		come	
swim		hurry		skip	
fill		hope		scare	
please		live		love	
try		chop		transfer	
hop		beg		shake	

Looking back and making connections
On the back of this sheet, list what sort of safety rules and equipment you would have if you had a pool in your backyard.

BLM 2 Queen of the Pool

1 Use the clues to complete this word puzzle.

1 The name of the main character.
2 Selena's family moved to a n_ _ house.
3 Selena's brother's name.
4 Selena was a _ _ _ _ _ of water.
5 Jade nearly d_ _ _ _ _ _.
6 The pool g_ _ _ was left open.
7 Selena's dad was transferred because he got a p_ _ _ _ _ _ _ _.
8 Selena jumped in the pool to r_ _ _ _ _ Jade.
9 Selena decided to learn to s_ _ _.
10 One of the safety measures was a blow-up r _ _ _.
11 Selena's brother said that she could be in the Olympic G_ _ _ _.

2 List the safety measures that Selena's parents took after Jade nearly drowned.

a. ________________________

b. ________________________

c. ________________________

3 Fill in the table to show how Selena changed in the story.

What Selena was like at the beginning of the story.	What Selena was like at the end of the story.

4 On the other side of this sheet, design a water safety poster.

BLM 1 The Creature of Cassidy's Creek

1 *Prepositions* are words that tell where something is or where something happens. In the sentences below, underline the group of words that tell where the action happens, then circle the preposition. The first example has been done for you.

a He heard a noise that came from the cellar.

b There was something behind the hidey-hole door.

c There was a sliding bolt on the door.

d A strange smell came up from the cellar.

e Sebastian heard a noise and jumped out of bed and stood beside the door.

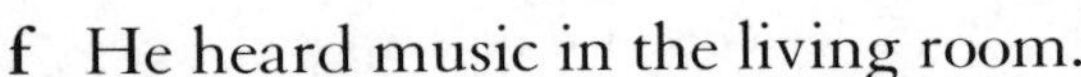

f He heard music in the living room.

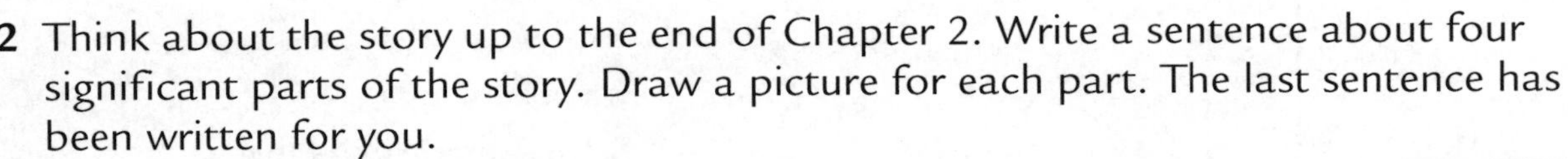

2 Think about the story up to the end of Chapter 2. Write a sentence about four significant parts of the story. Draw a picture for each part. The last sentence has been written for you.

	Sebastian is running back to bed.

Looking back and making connections
What would you do to find out what is making the noise? Why might Gran not hear the noise? Use the other side of this sheet to write your answers.

BLM 2 The Creature of Cassidy's Creek

1 Use the clues to complete this crossword.

Across

3 Sebastian threw a _ _ _ _ a u l i n over the possum.
5 Sebastian and Gran used this to trick the possum into the cage.
6 These were hanging crookedly at the window.
7 Sebastian climbed this.
10 The movement in the window still remained a m _ _ _ _ _ y.
11 This had bites in it.
13 The creature that made the noise.

Down

1 The type of noise Sebastian heard.
2 The sort of house Gran lived in.
4 Where the possum was released.
8 Where the noise first came from.
9 Sebastian saw two of these when he entered the cellar.
12 What was tipped over on the sideboard.

2 Adverbs are used to describe verbs. Form an adverb from the base word to complete the sentences below. The first example has been done for you.

a Sebastian (quick) ___quickly___ slid the bolt across the door of the cellar.

b Sebastian woke (sudden) ____________ in the middle of the night.

c The jangle of music (abruptly) ____________ stopped.

d The door to the cellar was (tight) __________ locked.

e Sebastian (hurry) _____________ mopped up the water from the vase.

BLM 1 MacTavish's Creature

1 List all the things that made Alex and Brendan suspicious of the new neighbours.

____
____
____
____
____
____

2 Complete this table by adding the comparative and superlative forms of the adjectives listed below.

Adjective	Comparative	Superlative
large		
strange		
odd		
sad		
merry		
happy		
scary		
tiny		
good		

3 Add the appropriate form of the adjective to these sentences. The first example has been done for you.

a Alex was ____braver____ (brave) than Brendan.

b The boys saw the ______________ (weird) furniture they had ever seen.

c The van driver carried an ______________ (odd) thing down the ramp.

d The noise was ______________ (scary) than anything they had heard before.

e Dr and Mrs MacTavish did not seem like ______________ (ordinary) neighbours to Alex.

f Alex had the ______________ (strange) imagination.

Looking back and making connections
Think about Alex's reactions to and opinions of the new neighbours. On the other side of this sheet, write what people could do to welcome and get to know new neighbours.

BLM 2 MacTavish's Creature

1 Read the clues below and find the words in the word search puzzle. Write the words you find at the side of the puzzle.

i	y	a	A	l	e	x	i	l	i	m	g	p
s	k	e	l	e	t	o	n	n	c	e	n	d
m	k	j	o	y	S	c	o	t	l	a	n	d
b	a	c	k	y	a	r	d	o	j	o	y	o
a	w	a	t	l	a	a	t	r	w	a	i	c
g	t	m	q	e	t	t	w	t	q	e	t	t
p	f	e	n	c	e	e	k	u	t	w	k	o
i	w	r	w	a	i	q	f	r	z	e	z	r
p	f	a	t	l	a	w	a	i	l	i	n	g
e	e	t	f	w	a	i	q	n	j	r	t	l
s	c	a	r	e	d	e	t	g	g	d	e	t
e	t	l	a	d	d	i	e	s	t	l	a	t
n	e	i	g	h	b	o	u	r	s	p	g	l
m	h	z	i	f	c	r	e	a	t	u	r	e
w	f	f	l	a	u	g	h	e	d	t	l	g
f	B	r	e	n	d	a	n	q	t	p	g	l

1 ____________
2 ____________
3 ____________
4 ____________
5 ____________
6 ____________
7 ____________
8 ____________
9 ____________
10 ____________
11 ____________
12 ____________
13 ____________
14 ____________
15 ____________
16 ____________
17 ____________
18 ____________

1 The name of the main character
2 Alex's friend's name
3 What we call people who live next to or near each other
4 This is what the boys thought made the noise
5 The country the new neighbours came from
6 Where the boys camped for the night
7 Dr MacTavish's occupation
8 This is the noise the creature made
9 These made the noise
10 This is what the boys thought Dr MacTavish was doing to the creature
11 A word for strange or odd
12 What the boys did when Dr MacTavish showed them the bagpipes
13 The bony frame of a body
14 The boys climbed over this
15 What Dr MacTavish called the boys
16 How the boys felt when they heard the noise
17 What the boys used to take a photo
18 A word for easily broken

2 On the other side of this sheet, make your own word search puzzle about the story to share with a friend.

BLM 1 A Medal for Molly

1 Complete these sentences by adding the reason for each action.

a Molly had visited her grandma because ______________________

____

b Molly's mother didn't go because ______________________

____

c A service station attendant had told Molly's dad about a short cut because ______________________

____

d Molly's father rang Molly's mother on the service station telephone because ______________________

____

e Molly's dad was annoyed at the service station attendant because ______________________

____

f The car crashed because ______________________

____

g Molly's dad couldn't move because ______________________

____

2 Use a dictionary to complete this table. Then write a sentence about the story that includes the word.

drowsy		
reduce		
jolt		
impact		

Looking back and making connections
On the other side of this sheet, write what you would do first in a situation like this.

BLM 2 A Medal for Molly

1 Read each statement below. Write the sentences from the story that give this information.

a Molly lived in the country. (p.4) ______________________

____

b Molly's dad felt responsible for the accident. (p.18) ______________________

____

c Molly had a way of helping herself overcome her fears. (p.22) ______________________

____

d Molly was delighted to see a house. (p.25) ______________________

____

e Molly had walked a very long way. (p.29) ______________________

____

f Molly was unselfish and modest. (p.32)

____

____

____

____

2 The apostrophe of possession is used to show that something or someone belongs to someone. Add the apostrophe of possession to the statements below. Underline the name of the owner. The first example has been done for you.

The dad belonging to Molly.	Molly's dad
The birthday belonging to Grandma.	
The suggestion belonging to the service station attendant.	
The side belonging to the car.	
The legs belonging to Dad.	
The barks belonging to two dogs.	
The clothes belonging to the daughter.	
The car belonging to the woman.	
The ambulance belonging to the ambulance officers.	

BLM 1 The Trouble with Oatmeal

1 Sort these words into groups according to their letter patterns. The first three words have been sorted for you.

deciduous, contagious, dangerous, serious, disastrous, furious, famous, curious, conscious, sensuous, luxurious, joyous, tempestuous

decid**uous**	contag**ious**	danger**ous**

2 Use a dictionary to find the meanings of these words.

disastrous ____________________

conscious ____________________

tempestuous ____________________

3 List what you know about each of these characters.

Lucy	Tree

Looking back and making connections
Use the other side of this sheet to write a letter to either Lucy or Tree. Ask them questions that you would like answered.

BLM 2 The Trouble with Oatmeal

1 Dashes are used to join two parts of a sentence. Choose the correct ending from the box below to complete these sentences. Refer to the text to check your answers.

she wants to meet you.
like her cat, and my little brother.
all the envelopes were addressed to me!
that's supposed to help her settle into her new home.

a We'd always sat together at school, and we'd shared our 'special' things — ____________________ (p.8)

b And guess what — ____________________ (p.9)

c Mum put butter on her paws — ____________________ (p.14)

d She thinks you sound cool — ____________________ (p.18)

2 Re-write these sentences and insert a dash.

a Help I've just seen a kid next door! (p.17) ____________________

b He's not bad for a boy! (p.21) ____________________

c WHEW were we glad to see him!!! (p.26) ____________________

d Then I saw something wriggle something small, and grey. (p.31) ____________________

3 Both Oatmeal and Brady escaped and were thought to be lost. Compare their experiences.

	Oatmeal	Brady
How they escaped		
What people did to find them		
Where they were found		

BLM 1 The Junkyard Dog

1 The sentences below contain information that can be found by reading 'between the lines'. Write the sentences from the text that give this information.

a The dog wasn't well looked after. (p.5) ______________________

____

____

b I didn't want anyone to know that I was feeding a dog. (p.6) ______________________

____

____

c Prince did not like what Stewart was doing. (p.9) ______________________

____

____

2 Rewrite the verbs in the brackets in the past tense.

a Rachel __________ (hears) a loud noise.

b The dog __________ (barks) loudly.

c Stewart _______ (is) annoying Prince.

d Stewart ______ (is) kicking the fence

and Prince ______ (is) flinging himself against it.

e Rachel _______ (yells) at Stewart

and he ________ (kicks) the fence again.

3 If you could ask three questions of Rachel, what would they be? Make sure that the questions help you understand the character or story better.

____

____

____

Looking back and making connections
Use the other side of this sheet to write what you thought about Stewart's actions. If you had to tell someone how to look after a dog, what would you say?

BLM 2 The Junkyard Dog

1 Read each sentence and tick a box to show whether it uses direct or reported speech. The first example has been done for you.

	reported speech	direct speech
a Coach said that there would be no swimming for Rachel.	✓	
b "But I'll miss the final selection," cried Rachel.		
c Coach said, "I'm sorry. But breathing like that, you're not going to win anyway."		
d Rachel said that Prince had saved her life.		
e "You'll be in the team next time," Coach said to Rachel.		

2 Read the passages below. Write the information you find from reading *between the lines*.

a The time for the swimming sports drew nearer. I was in bed every night before nine. In the morning I did exercises, and every afternoon Prince came with me to the pool.

____

____

b Stewart did come to the pool. Coach took one look and said, "You. In the water. Down at the shallow end. And do what I say." ______________________

____

c I felt something dragging at my shirt. My head went under again. I don't remember any more. ______________________

____

3 Think of the best adjective to describe each character and add your reason for choosing it.

a Rachel was ______________ because ______________________

____

b Stewart was ______________ because ______________________

____

c Coach was ______________ because ______________________

____

Looking back and making connections
On the back of this sheet, write a newspaper report about how Prince saved Rachel.

BLM 1 Super-Tuned!

1 Insert the punctuation marks in these sentences. Then add a better word than 'said'.

a I still don't see why I have to wear a hearing aid he ________________ .

b It will help you at school Nick his mum ____________________ .

c Did you get it Adrian _______ .

d What'll we do this afternoon ___________________ Adrian.

e You can't wear someone else's hearing aid _________________ Nick.

2 Answer the questions. Use complete sentences.

a How did Nick feel when he first got his hearing aid? ____________________

____

b What did Nick think the people at school would do when they saw his hearing aid? ____

____

c What did Adrian think about Nick's hearing aid? ____________________

____

d What were some of the things Nick could hear with his hearing aid? ____________

____

3 In *contractions,* an apostrophe shows that a letter or letters have been left out of the word. Complete this table. The first example has been done for you.

Contraction	Expanded words	Contraction	Expanded words
we'll	we will	there's	
what'll		can't	
it's		isn't	
won't		didn't	
I'll		they're	
you'd		wasn't	
we're		don't	
I'm		you're	

Looking back and making connections.
Nick said that he could have fun with his hearing aid. Think creatively, and use the other side of this sheet to list all the fun things you could do with his hearing aid.

BLM 2 Super-Tuned!

1 *Conjunctions* are used to join sentences and parts of sentences. Add a conjunction to join the sentences below and change the punctuation. The first example has been done for you. Refer to the book to check your answers.

a He turned the sound right down. ___so___ He he didn't hear the radio signals. (p.12)

b He took it off. __________ He handed it to her. (p.12)

c The teacher explained that Nick needed a hearing aid. __________ His ear had been damaged from having lots of ear infections. (p.13)

d They're in danger. __________ I think I am the only one who can hear them, through my hearing aid. (p.17)

e The storm had begun to ease. __________ Nick could see that the ocean was still rough. (p.24)

2 Choose words from the following list and match them to the words in the table below. The first example has been done for you.

answered ***moaned*** ***whispered*** ***asked*** ***cried*** ***shouted***

yelled	murmured	groaned	replied	inquired	whimpered
shouted					

3 Fill in the missing words to complete this flow chart of the story.

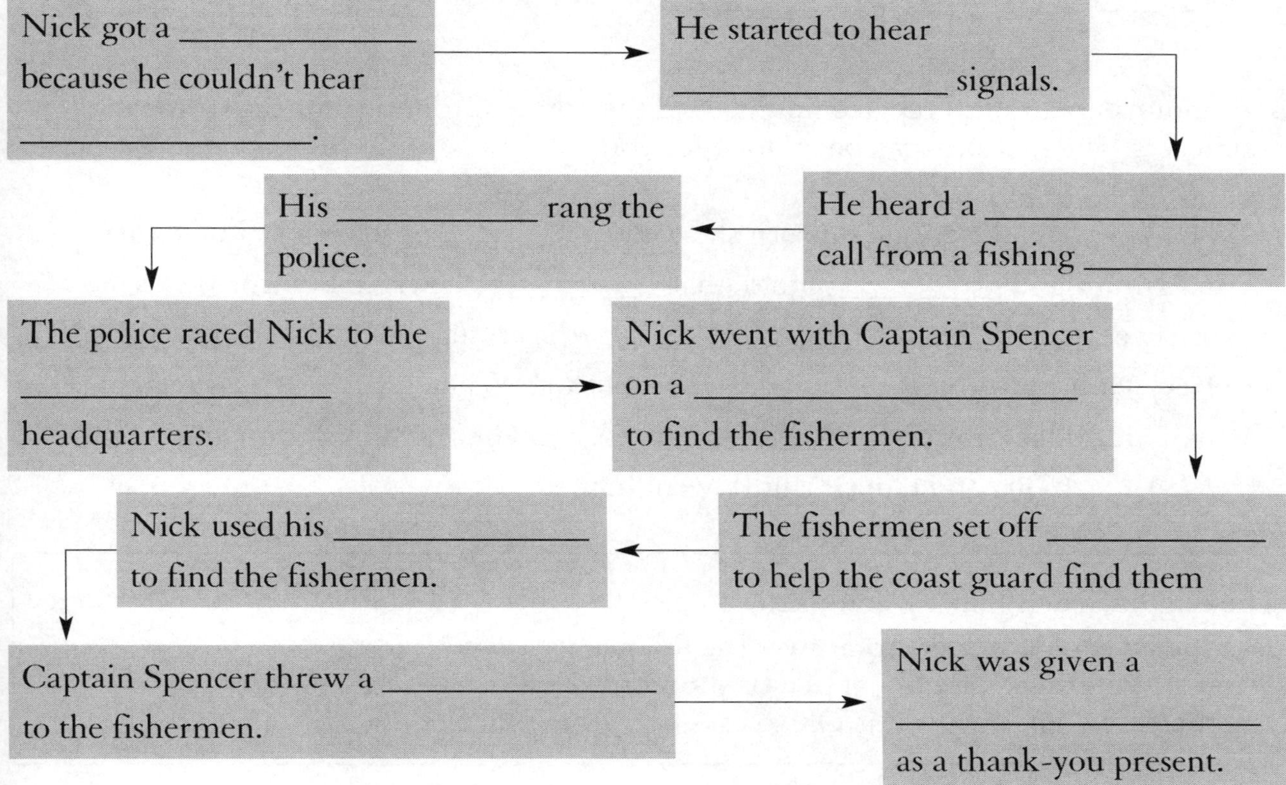

BLM 1 The Crystal Unicorn

1 Find the meaning of these words. (*Uni* means *one*.)
Then find some other words beginning with *Uni*.

Word	Meaning
unicorn	
unicycle	
universe	
university	

2 This story is written in the first person, from the point of view of Gina. Add the personal pronouns that indicate that she is telling the story. The first one has been done for you. Refer to the book.

___We___ went home on the train , and that's when the trouble started — everyone on _________ seat was so squashed together that the unicorn began to poke into _________ side. If it was paid for, _________ thought, it would be wrapped in tissue paper. And it would be in a carry bag so it couldn't hurt _________ .
But _________ *hadn't* paid for the unicorn. And _________ would have to wait till _________ got home before _________ could even look at it again. (pages 8–9)

3 Pronouns are used to replace nouns. Add the correct pronouns for the words in brackets. The first one has been done for you.

When Gina saw the crystal unicorn she wanted ____it____ .(the crystal unicorn) Gina's mum told _________(Gina) that _________ (the crystal unicorn) was expensive._________ (Gina) took _________ (the crystal unicorn) and put _________ (the crystal unicorn) in _________ (Gina's) pocket. When _________ (Gina and Gina's Mum) had finished _________ (Gina's and Gina's Mum's) shopping _________ (Gina and Gina's Mum) went home.

Looking back and making connections
Use the back of this sheet to answer the following:
What do you think should happen to shoplifters?
Are there any times when it is OK to take something that doesn't belong to you?

BLM 2 The Crystal Unicorn

1 There are many reasons for the actions in this story. Complete these sentences:

a Gina stole the crystal unicorn because ______________________________

____

b Gina took it back to the jeweller because ____________________________

____

c The jeweller didn't call the police because ___________________________

____

d Gina did a lot of work for other people because _______________________

____

2 Choose three words from the box to describe Gina. Write them in the spaces. Then write examples from the story of when Gina was like this.

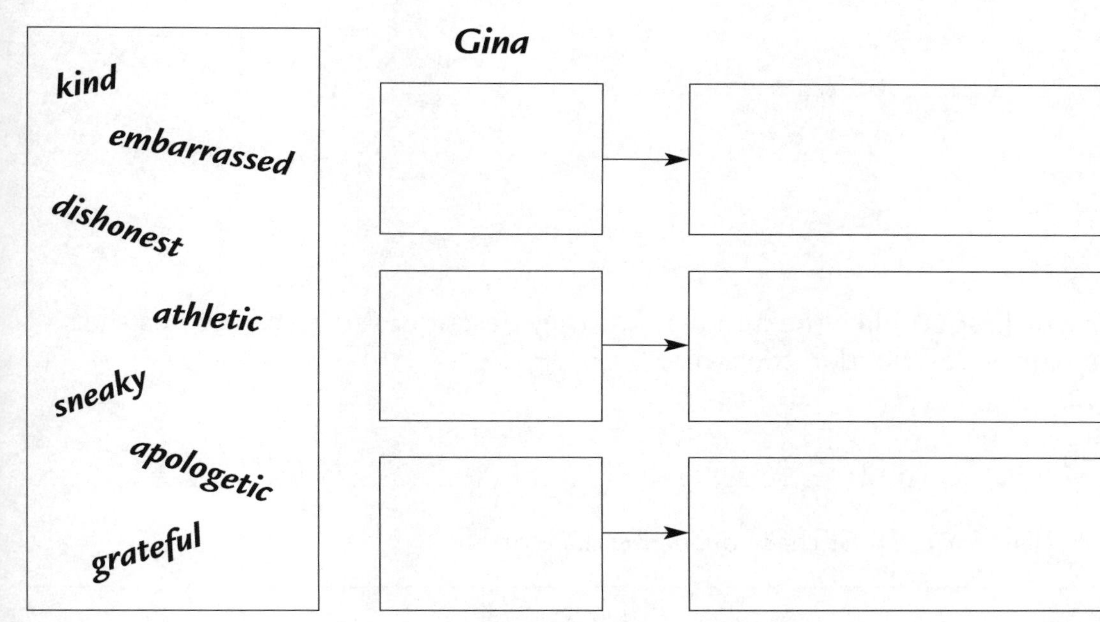

3 Add the punctuation marks to these sentences. Refer to the book to check your answers.

a What kind of glass is this I asked Mum (page 4)
b Whats the matter Gina she asked (page 14)
c Yes I said softly I'll have to take it back (page 15)
d I could put it on lay-by for you Mum said Then the jeweller puts it away until all the payments are made (page 24)

BLM 1 Alfred the Curious

1 Draw a line connecting the characters with their actions. Circle the *auxiliary verb* and underline the verb. The first example has been done for you.

Characters	Actions
People	were getting their lances.
Foot soldiers	were winching the drawbridge up.
The archers	were running.
The children	were coming after Lord Edward.
The two lords	were racing up the stairs.
Lord William and his army	had been fighting over the castle for a long time.
Alfred	were being hurried inside.
The gatehouse keepers	was running down the spiral stairs.

2 Find the meanings of these words.

a parapet ____________________

____

b squire ____________________

____

c archers ____________________

____

3 *Onomatopoeic* words sound like the actions that they describe. Write the actions that the following words described in the story.

a Thud … Thud … (p.12) ____________________

b Thwat … Thwat … (p.12) ____________________

4 Write a description for each of these *onomatopoeic* words.

quack		bang	
hiss		boom	
miaow		whoosh	

5 On the other side of this sheet, draw a map of the castle and add labels from the list below.

spiral staircase, parapet, slits in tower wall, tower, drawbridge, winch, stables, gatehouse, courtyard, pens, storeroom, castle walls

Looking back and making connections
Life was very different in the time when Alfred lived. What would be the advantages of living during that time? What would be the disadvantages of living during that time?

BLM 2 Alfred the Curious

1 Choose the correct *auxiliary verb* from the box to complete these sentences.

shall	have	do	must
will	has	does	would
are	had	should	were
was	could		

a Alfred ________ running down the stairs.

b Alfred and Bartholomew ________ heard a strange noise.

c Lord William and his army ________ coming after Lord Edward.

d The enemy ________ tunnelling under the castle.

e Bartholomew said that they ________ tell Lord Edward what ________ happening.

f Lord Edward thought of a plan that ________ defeat Lord William's army.

g Lord Edward ________ happy that they defeated Lord William's army.

2 Answer the questions. Use complete sentences.

a What did Lord William's army use to disguise the hut? (p.23) ________

____

b What did Alfred think about war? Why did he think this? (p.26) ________

____

____

c What were Alfred's plans for his future? (p.32) ________

____

3 Choose an appropriate word to describe each character and provide a reason to support your opinion.

a Alfred was ________ because ________

____

b Lord Edward was ________ because ________

____

c Bartholomew was ________ because ________

____

BLM 1 Yo-yos

1 Fill in the gaps with the name of the correct country. Refer to the text to check your answers.

a Yo-yos may have originated in ________________ . (p.5)

b In ______________, yo-yos were called *chuk chuks*. (p.6)

c Yo-yos were made from terracotta discs in ______________. (p.5)

d In ______________, yo-yos were mostly made from glass or ivory. (p.7)

e In ______________, children used buttons to make yo-yos. (p.14)

2 Use the information that you know about yo-yos to complete the table below.

Materials used to make yo-yos	Uses for yo-yos	Ways of decorating yo-yos

3 In your opinion, which country or countries seem to have taken the most interest in yo-yos? Why do you think this?

____

____

____

4 Conduct a PMI survey on yo-yos as toys. List the advantages (pluses), the disadvantages (minuses) and interesting facts about yo-yos.

Pluses	Minuses	Interesting facts

5 Use the other side of this sheet to draw a timeline showing the history and development of yo-yos.

BLM 2 Yo-yos

1 Use the information that you know about yo-yos to write the solutions in the table below.

Problem	Solution
The string is too tight.	
The string is too loose.	
The yo-yo string is too long.	
The string is frayed and worn.	
You are not good at using a yo-yo.	

2 Write the key words or information for each step in making a wooden yo-yo.

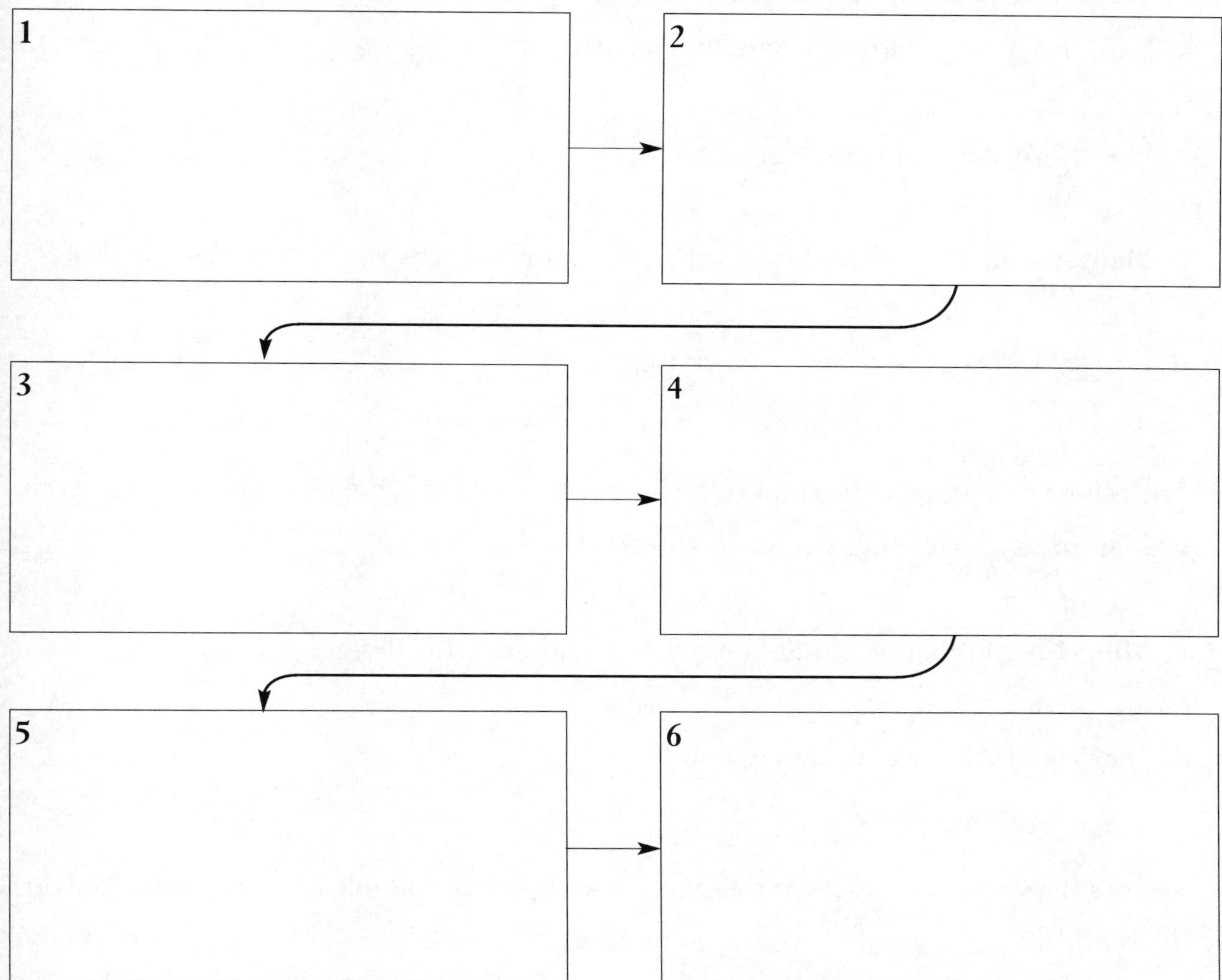

Looking back and making connections
Use the other side of this sheet to write about your experiences with yo-yos. Describe your favourite yo-yo, the tricks you can do, what you find easy or hard, and how you feel about yo-yos.

BLM 1 The Pushcart Team

1 Read the following sentences and tick the boxes to show whether they are true or false.

	true	false
a The pushcart race was part of the Greenmount Winter Festival.		
b Mrs Walipoor was Mansor's mother.		
c Amy's dad was reluctant to help them build the pushcart.		
d Amy believed the shape of the frame affects the strength of the pushcart.		
e Square shapes are stronger than triangular shapes.		

2 The following sentences use direct speech. Rewrite the sentences using reported speech.

a Ming-En asked, "How do you build a pushcart?" ____________________

____

b I said, "My dad can help." ____________________

____

c Mansor said, "Mum could help with wheels and other parts from her bicycle shop." _

____

d Dad said, "I suggest that you work together." ____________________

____

3 The following sentences use reported speech. Rewrite the sentences using direct speech.

a Mansor said that Ming-En was really good at drawing. ____________________

____

b Ming-En said that he didn't know if he could draw the design. ____________

____

c Dad asked what we wanted to build. ____________________

____

4 Rewrite the verbs in brackets in the past tense. The first example has been done for you.

The children ___*wanted*___ (want) to build a pushcart. They ____________ (speak) to people who ____________(tell) them how to make it. They ____________ (draw) a design and ____________ (show) it to Amy's father who ____________ (think) it ________ (is) good.

Looking back and making connections.
Use the back of this sheet to draw a bird's eye view of the following: your table, the rubbish bin, the chair, your bedroom.

BLM 2 The Pushcart Team

1 Use words from the list below to add labels to the picture of the pushcart. One example has been done for you.

axle, wheels, steering rod, ball bearings, brake bracket, frame, pivot bolt, rope, seat, metal bolts, seatbelt, aluminium tubing

2 Add labels for any other parts that you know.

3 Around the pushcart, draw the safety gear and tools used in the text.

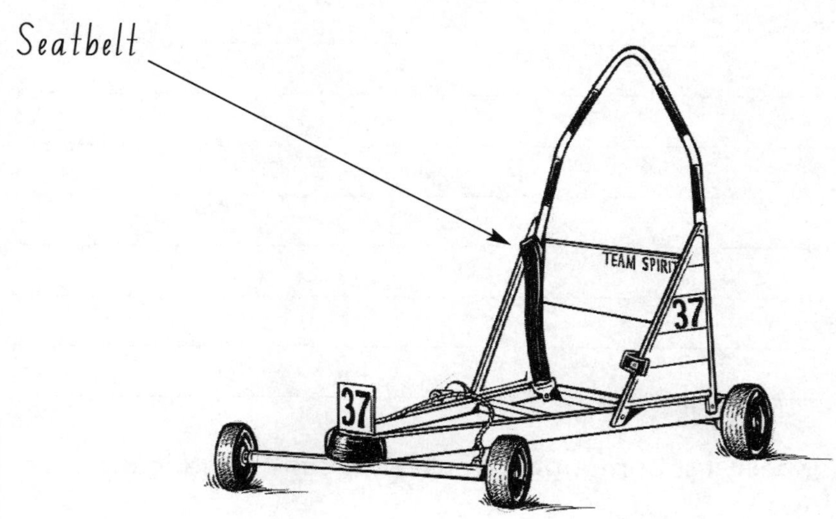

4 Use the other side of this sheet to write why tools and safety gear are important.

BLM 1 Snowboarding Diary

1 Find and list details from the text about each of the following items.

clothes	
jackets	
pants	
boots	
snowboards	
lodge	

2 Compound words are made up of two or more primary words that form a new word. Circle the primary words below and write the meaning of the new compound word. The first example has been done for you

snowboards	a board for the snow
airport	
skateboards	
waterproof	
chairlift	
lunchtime	
afternoon	
sideways	

4 On the other side of this sheet, list compound words that can be made up from the primary words listed below.

chalk foot table egg rain tooth tea gum gentle back screen green board house bow cloth cup boot man ball yard pot ache sun

5 Complete these sentences about snowboards to show cause and effect. Refer to the text to check your answers.

a A leash is attached to the board so ______________________

____

b Flexible wood bends so ______________________

____

c Each end is turned up slightly so ______________________

BLM 2 Snowboarding Diary

1 Choose key words from the list below, and write them as headings on the chart. The first example has been done for you.

skills, clothing, hats, chains, chairlift, attendant, leashes, heel turns, boots, snow-chains, equipment, gloves, instructor, people, stops, ski patrol, jackets, zigzag, bindings, snowboarders, toe turns, competitors, stunts

Snowboarding

SKILLS			
heel turns			

2 Use the back of this sheet to write or draw a safety poster for snowboarding.

BLM 1 Skateboarding

1 Answer these questions in complete sentences.

a What is the important difference between the two main types of skateboards? ______

b If you were going to skate on a ramp what type of skateboard would you use? ______

c Information about skateboards can be located on the Internet. Who would want this information and how could it help them? ______

d Who originally used skateboards in California and for what reasons? ______

2 Use the dictionary to help you complete this table.

Word	Meaning	A word that means the opposite
unique		
standard		
fantastic		
exactly		

3 The word *skateboard* is a *compound* word. Choose one word from the top row and combine it with one word from the bottom row to make a compound word. The first example has been done for you.

bread, light, ~~birth,~~ horse, every, some, card, moon, dough, web, wheel

nut, site, house, one, ~~day,~~ barrow, light, crumbs, shoe, where, board

birthday

Looking back and making connections

Use the other side of this sheet to write an argument supporting the need for people to wear safety clothing when they are skateboarding.

BLM 2 Skateboarding

1 Use the other side of this sheet to draw three columns. In the first column, write the facts from the newspaper report; in the second column, write Todd's point of view; and in the third column, write the librarian's point of view.

2 Use the information that you know about skateboards to complete this table.

	1960s	1970s	1980s	1990s	2000 →
Shape of board					
Material used					
Other equipment and clothing					
Places for skateboarding					

3 Use a different verb from the verbs in brackets to complete these sentences. Then write the past tense of the verbs in brackets in the box.

a (Choose) ___Select___ which foot will be at the front of the board. [chose]

b (Place) ____________ the other foot on the back of the board. [ ]

c (Push) ____________ yourself along with the back foot and then (put) ____________ it up on the board when you have (built) ____________ speed.
[ ] [ ] [ ]

d To (stop) ____________ just (put) ____________ your foot on the ground again.
[ ] [ ]

e (Practise) ____________ how to (keep) ____________ your balance on the board.
[ ] [ ]

4 Use the other side of this sheet to design the perfect skatepark.

BLM 1 Kites

1 Use the other side of this sheet to make a timeline, showing the development and use of kites.

2 Choose the correct homophone from the brackets to complete these sentences. The first example has been done for you.

a We will tell you a (tail, tale) ___tale___ about the (tail, tale) ___tail___ of a kite.

b Some Chinese (prince, prints) ____________ show people using kites.

c Kites have been used for (sum, some) ____________ important activities.

d Kites can fly (through, threw) ____________ the (air, heir) ____________.

e (Their, They're, There) ____________ are many kite festivals (where, wear) ____________ (ewe, you) ____________ can (see, sea) ____________ lots of kites.

3 Use a dictionary to help you complete this table.

Word	Meaning	Word that means the opposite
ancient		
original		
assistance		
attempt		

4 The words in the chart below have many different letter patterns that make the *e* sound. Find words with the same letter patterns on pp.5–9 that make the *e* sound. Add these words to the chart below. If you find any words with a different letter pattern for this sound, add them to the *other* column.

steep	be	Japanese	team	people	family	other

Looking back and making connections
Use the other side of this sheet to write a newspaper article that explains how the bridge over the river at Niagara Falls was built with the help of a kite.

BLM 2 Kites

1 Choose the correct word from the list below to complete these sentences.

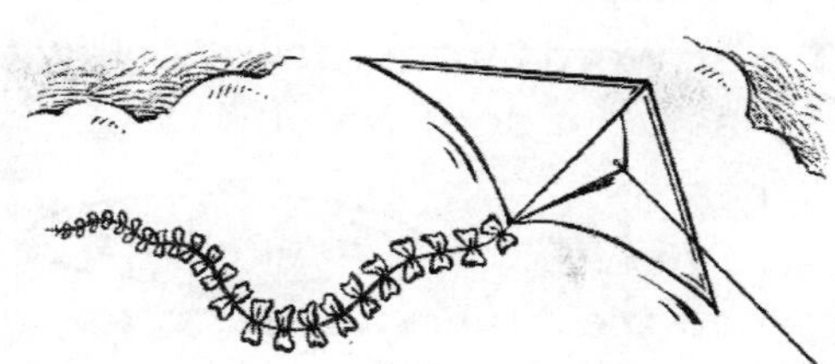

face, larger, strong, symmetrical, small, front, stable, lift

a The kite must be ________________ in shape if it is to fly well.

b The position of the tether point on a kite affects how much __________ the kite will get.

c The tail helps to keep the kite _________________ when it is flying. It also helps to make sure the _____________ of the kite is to the wind.

d The line has to be ____________ so that it doesn't break.

e For a kite to fly, air must press more on the ______________ of the kite than on the back.

f _____________ kites fly better in light winds and ______________ kites fly better in strong winds.

2 List some key words under the following headings.

Kites

History	***Uses***		***Parts of Kite***
	In the Past	***Now***	

Looking back and making connections.
Use the other side of this sheet to design a safety poster about kites. Visit the World Wide Web and make a list of *Further Fascinating Facts about Kites.*

BLM 1 The Bicycle Book

1 Use words from the list below to add labels to the picture of the bicycle. One example has been done for you.

saddle,	*handlebars,*	*brake lever,*	*front light,*	*back light,*
brake shoes,	*reflector,*	*chain,* *frame,*	*tyre,* *bell,*	*gear shifter,*
gear cable,	*valve cap,*		*packrack,*	*wheel rim*

2 Add labels for any other parts that you know.

3 Use the back of this sheet to list the clothing cyclists can wear and other kinds of safety equipment that can be added to a bicycle.

BLM 2 The Bicycle Book

1 Add numbers to indicate the correct order of the steps for changing a tyre. Underline the verbs. The first step has been done for you.

	Put the new tube inside the tyre.
	Pull out the inner tube.
	Pump up the tyre.
	Tuck the tyre back inside the wheel rim.
	Pinch the tyre walls together to separate the tyre from the wheel rim.
1	<u>Unscrew</u> the valve cap.
	Push the valve back through the hole in the rim.
	Push the valve to deflate the tyre.
	Unhook one side of the tyre from the wheel.

2 Write the purpose of each of the items below. Check your answers on p.8–9 of the text.

Item	Purpose
reflectors	
bell	
bike pump	
drink bottle	
pannier	

3 Write the solution to each problem. Check your answers in the text.

Problem	Solution
When car doors open in front of a cyclist (p.15)	
When you are unsure how to cross a busy intersection (p.17)	
When there is no bike path or bike route (p.16)	
When the bike squeaks while you pedal (p.26)	

4 Use the dictionary to find the meaning of these words.

lubricate ______________________________

dehydrated ______________________________

straddle ______________________________

grate ______________________________

BLM 1 Funny Business

1 Fill in the missing information. The first example has been done for you.

First speaker	Second speaker
Can I have a dog?	*No, you can't have a dog.*
	No, the dog can not sleep on your bed.
	Yes, it would be funny seeing the dog chase Mrs Sims down the road.
	Yes, you could feed him vegetables.
Will you pretend to be my dog?	

2 Write the *literal meaning* for the common sayings below.

a *Butterflies in your stomach* means ____________________

b *Two left feet* means ____________________

c *To turn over a new leaf* means ____________________

d *Down in the mouth* means ____________________

e *In the same boat* means ____________________

3 Find the words used in the text to describe the actions listed below.

Action	Words used in the text
ran (pp.10, 13, 18)	
pushed (pp.11, 13)	
said (pp.12, 18, 23)	
looked (pp.12, 21, 22, 23)	

Looking back and making connections
Use the other side of this sheet to write about the part of the anthology that you enjoyed the most. Why did you enjoy this part?

BLM 2 Funny Business

1 Reread the fiction stories in the anthology and fill in the following table.

Title	Text type	Who was telling the story?	Main character	The problem	My thoughts about the story

2 List all the information that you know about anthologies.

List of computer task centre activity cards

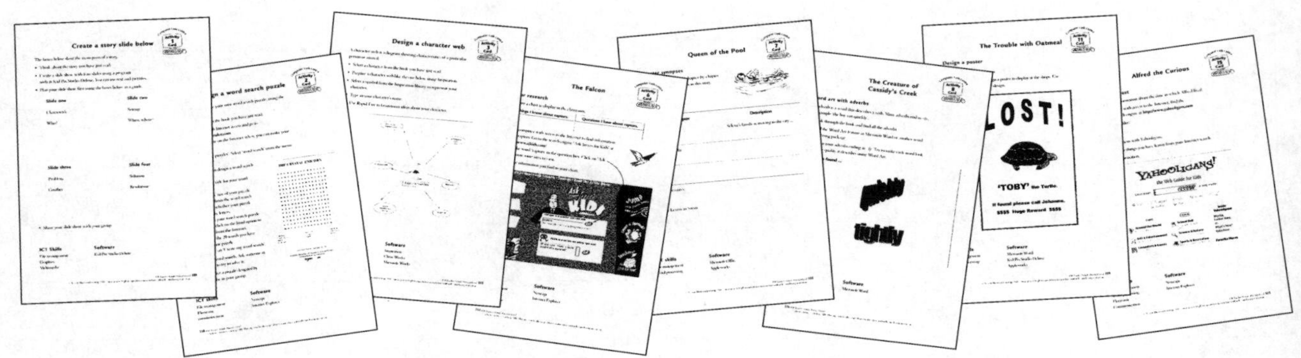

Create a story slide show

The boxes below show the main parts of a story.

- Think about the story you have just read.
- Create a slide show with four slides using a program such as Kid Pix Studio Deluxe. You can use text and pictures.
- Plan your slide show first using the boxes below as a guide.

Slide one

Character/s

Who?

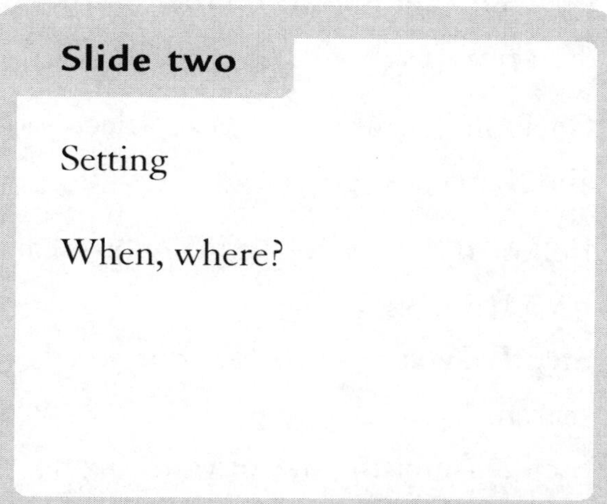

Slide two

Setting

When, where?

Slide three

Problem

Conflict

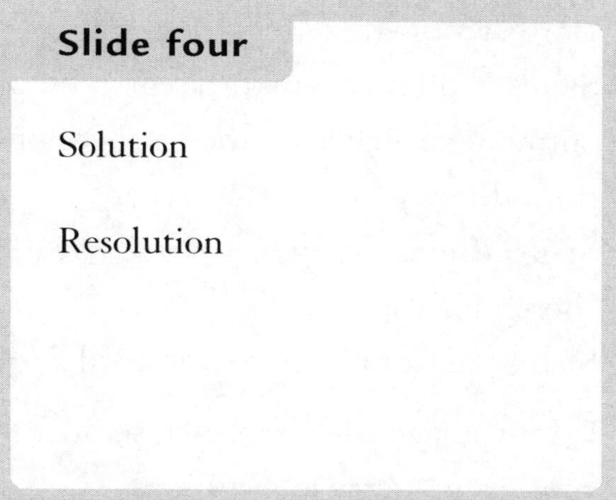

Slide four

Solution

Resolution

- Share your slide show with your group.

ICT Skills

File management
Graphics
Multimedia

Software

Kid Pix Studio Deluxe

Design a word search puzzle

Follow the steps to make your own word search puzzle, using the Internet.

- Select 20 words from the book you have just read.
- Use a computer with Internet access and go to **http://www.puzzlemaker.com**
  Puzzlemaker is a site on the Internet where you can make your own puzzles.
- Click on 'try other puzzles'. Select 'word search' from the menu and then click 'go'.
- Follow the steps to design a word search for a friend.
  Step 1 Type in a title for your word search.
  Step 2 Enter the size of your puzzle.
  Step 3 Choose from the word search puzzle options whether your puzzle words will share letters.
  Step 4 Choose your word search puzzle output type – click on the html option to print directly from the Internet.
  Step 5 Enter the 20 words you have chosen for your puzzle.
  Step 6 Click on 'Create my word search'.
- Print your word search. Ask someone in your group to try to solve it.
- Try and solve a puzzle designed by someone else in your group.

THE CRYSTAL UNICORN

Y P F B E Q A C T D B L L L A
S T W T Q Y X B T X K A S R P
C U I F V A P V B K N T B J M
R S C I T S A N M Y G S C A S
B E B P R Z P E C X R Y E C B
E U L H N O Q C A A A R O K H
M Q Z L L R U R L F F C S E J
D X B I E T U L D Y C W E T P
W R C M Q W O U N I C O R N Q
A E A T B D E Z M Y R S T G C
Y X P W I F P J U I U N N Y T
O A V O E E G H F K M F X F O
L F Q L H R O O N I T A T H D
N I A R T S D P K D G E A J T
M D F S F I P V H T S R J F O

CRYSTAL
GYMNASTICS
POLICE
UNICORN
DOLLARS
JACKET
SHOP
DRAWER
JEWELLER
TRAIN

Solution / How to Save Your Puzzle

Visit Puzzlemaker at Discovery Channel School
www.discoveryschool.com
DiscoverySchool.com

ICT skills

File management
Electronic communication

Software

Netscape
Internet Explorer

Design a character web

A character web is a diagram showing characteristics of a particular person or animal.

- Select a character from the book you have just read.
- Prepare a character web like the one below using Inspiration.
- Select a symbol from the Inspiration library to represent your character.
- Type in your character's name.
- Use Rapid Fire to brainstorm ideas about your character.

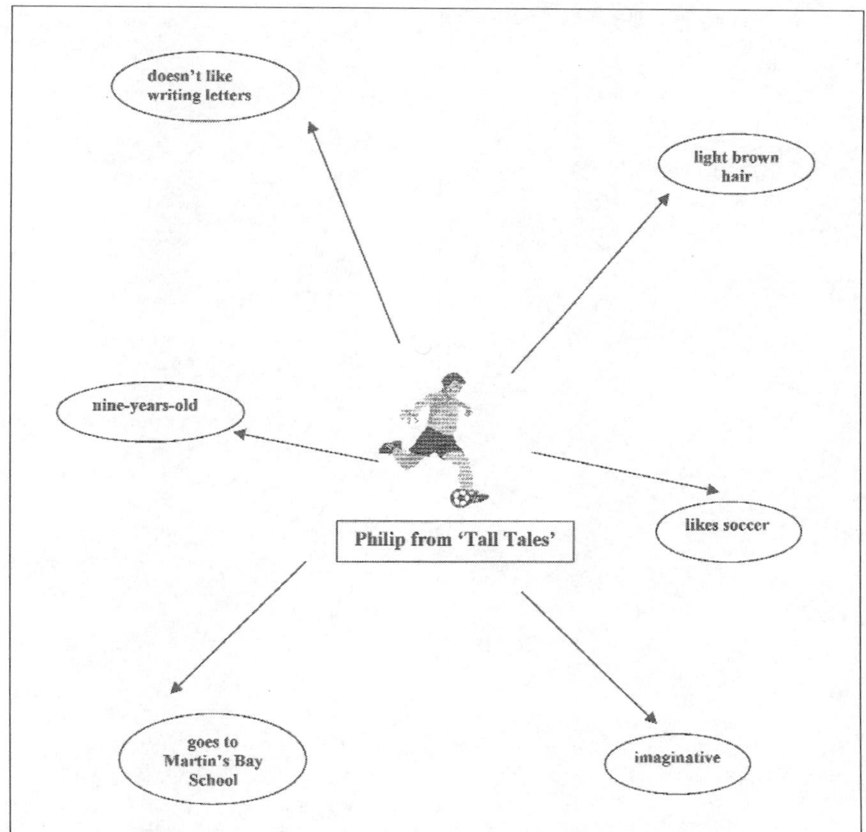

ICT skills

File management
Word processing
Graphics

Software

Inspiration
Claris Works
Microsoft Works

Tall Tales

Tall tale or truth?

Think about the information in Philip and Anna's letters. What information was true and what was a tall tale?

- Set up a table like the one below in a program of your choice. For instance, you could use Kid Pix Studio Deluxe, Microsoft Office or Appleworks.

Truth	Tall Tale

ICT skills

File management
Word processing

Software

Kid Pix Studio Deluxe
Microsoft Office
Appleworks

The Secret

Character focus

- Think about the two characters Chris and Andrew. What do you know about each boy?
- Use Kid Pix Studio Deluxe to create a slide show with four slides.
- Plan your slide show first using the topics below.

Slide one

Character: Chris

Slide two

What I know about the character

Slide three

Character: Andrew

Slide four

What I know about the character

- Save your slide show.
- Share your slide show with the group.

ICT skills

File management
Graphics
Multimedia

Software

Kid Pix Studio Deluxe

The Falcon

Raptor research

- Prepare a chart to display in the classroom.

Things I know about raptors.	Questions I have about raptors.

- Use a computer with access to the Internet to find information about raptors. Go to the search engine 'Ask Jeeves for Kids' at **http://www.ajkids.com/**
  Type the word 'raptors' in the question box. Click on 'Ask' and choose some sites to view.
- Add the information you find to your chart.

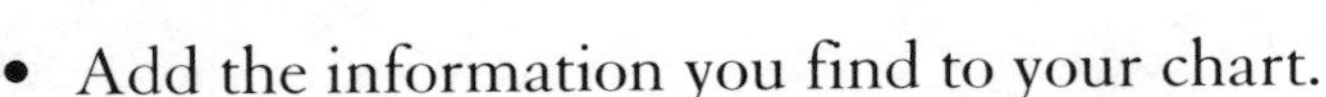

ICT skills

File management
Electronic communication

Software

Netscape
Internet Explorer

Queen of the Pool

Chapter synopses

Use a computer to write a chapter-by-chapter description of what happens in this story.

Chapter	Description
1 The Promotion	Selena's family is moving to the city ...
2 Selena Settles In	
3 The Hero	
4 Safety Measures	
5 Selena Learns to Swim	

ICT skills

File management
Word processing

Software

Microsoft Office
Appleworks

The Creature of Cassidy's Creek

Word art with adverbs

An adverb is a word that describes a verb. Many adverbs end in *–ly*, for example 'the boy ran quickly'.

- Look through the book and find all the adverbs.
- Find the Word Art feature in Microsoft Word or another word processing package.
- Type in your adverbs ending in *–ly*. Try to make each word look like the quality it describes using Word Art.

Adverbs found ...

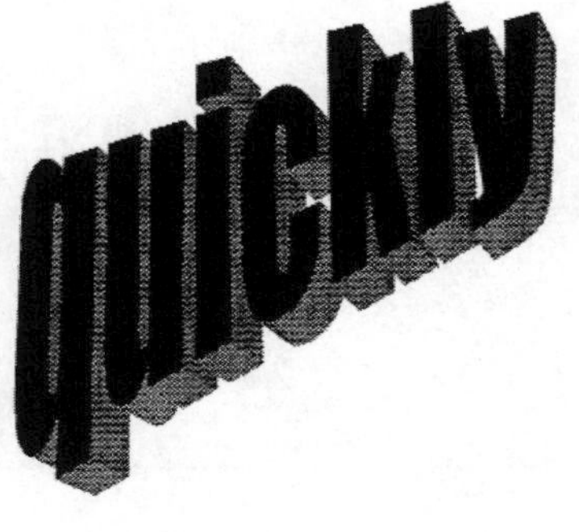

ICT skills

File management
Word processing
Graphics

Software

Microsoft Word

MacTavish's Creature

Cast of characters

- Choose three characters from the story.
- Write a description of each character.
- Draw each character using Kid Pix Studio Deluxe. Select 'Paint a picture' and use the drawing tools to draw each character.
- Save each picture to make a slide show.
- Share your 'cast of characters' with the group.

Alex from *MacTavish's Creature*.

ICT skills

File management
Graphics
Multimedia

Software

Kid Pix Studio Deluxe

A Medal for Molly

Feelings graph

- Think about how Molly's feelings changed in the different chapters of this book.
- Make a graph or chart using a program like Appleworks or Microsoft Excel.
- How did Molly feel:
  – on the trip home?
  – when the crash happened?
  – when no one came to help?
  – when she was searching for help?
  – when help came?

Record Molly's feelings on a graph like the one below.

"A Medal for Molly"

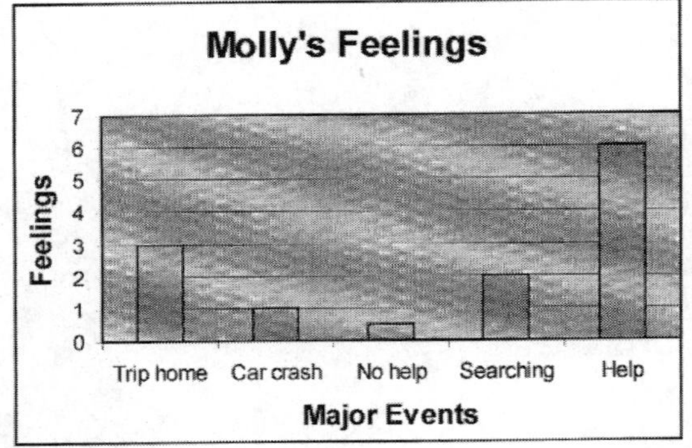

Key

0 = Absolutely terrible	**3 = OK**
0.5 = Really awful	**4 = A bit better**
1 = Very sad	**5 = Happy**
2 = Sad	**6 = Ecstatic!**

ICT skills

File management
Word processing
Graphics

Software

Appleworks
Microsoft Excel

The Trouble with Oatmeal

Design a poster

- Pretend you have lost a pet.
- Use the computer to design a poster to display at the shops. Use graphics and text in your design.

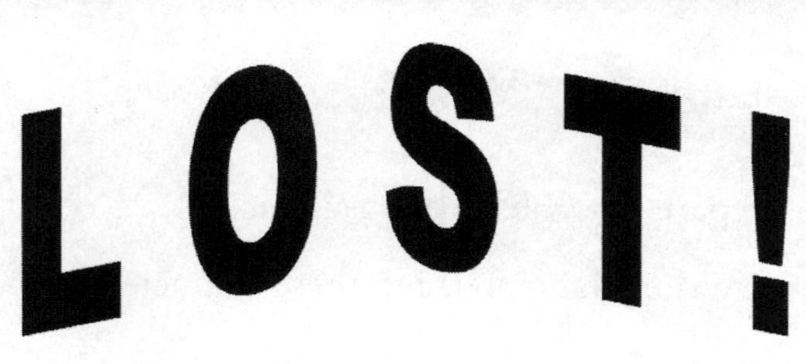

'TOBY' **the Turtle.**

If found please call Johanna.

$$$$ Huge Reward $$$$

ICT skills

File management
Word processing
Graphics

Software

Microsoft Word
Kid Pix Studio Deluxe
Appleworks

The Junkyard Dog

Character profile

The main characters in the story are:

Prince

Rachel

Stewart

Coach

- Use the computer to prepare a profile of these characters.
- After reading the story, write what you think these characters are really like.

Prince	**Rachel**
Stewart	**Coach**

ICT skills

File management
Word processing

Software

Microsoft Office
Appleworks
Kid Pix Studio Deluxe

Super-Tuned!

Retell the story

- Scan the cover of *Super-Tuned!*.
- Insert the scanned image into a program like Kid Pix Studio Deluxe, Microsoft Office, or Appleworks.
- Retell the story in your own words.

Retell the story here.

This is a story about a boy who got a new hearing aid. He could pick up radio signals in his ears. One day he heard a distress signal from a sinking ship. He was able to lead the rescue team to the ship by listening to the signals. The crew was saved. The boy was given a 'thank you' present—and a new hearing aid!

ICT skills

File management
Word processing
Graphics

Software

Kid Pix Studio Deluxe
Microsoft Office
Appleworks

Hardware

Scanner

The Crystal Unicorn

Character focus

- Set up a grid like the one below, using a computer.

Pluses	Minuses	Ideas

- Complete a **PMI** (pluses, minuses and ideas grid) about what Gina did in this story.
- Share your PMI with your partner

ICT skills

File management
Word processing

Software

Microsoft Office
Appleworks

Alfred the Curious

Research the past

- Find out more information about the time in which Alfred lived.
- Using a computer with access to the Internet, find the Yahooligans search engine at **http://www.yahooligans.com**
- Key in words like 'castle' and 'knight' and click on 'search' to view.
- Record five new things you have learnt from your Internet search.
- Share your information.

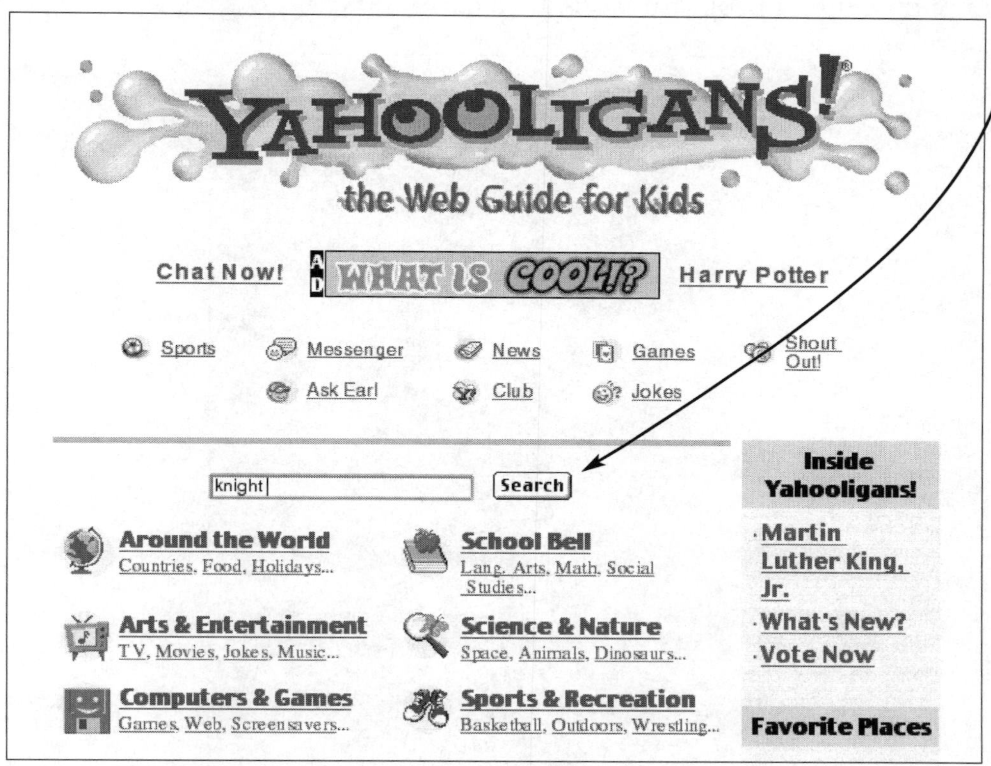

ICT skills

File management
Word processing
Electronic
Communication

Software

Netscape
Internet Explorer

Yo-yos

Make a book

- Bring a yo-yo to school.
- Reread Chapter 6 of *Yo-yos*, and try out some of these tricks:
  The Spinner
  Walk the Dog
  Around the World
  Rock the Baby.
- Take some digital photos of your friends trying the yo-yo tricks.
- Insert the photos into a program to create a class book.

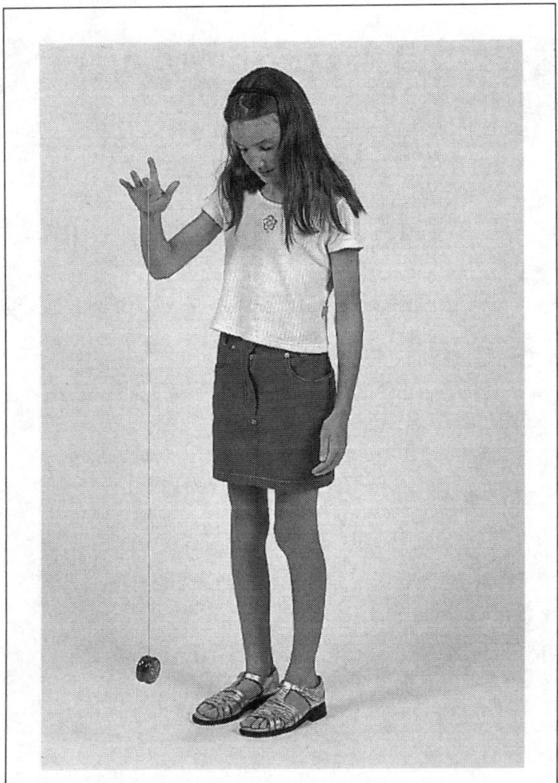

This is Selena trying *The Spinner*.

ICT skills

File management
Graphics
Multimedia

Software

Microsoft Office
Appleworks
Kid Pix Studio Deluxe

Hardware

Digital camera

The Pushcart Team

Design and draw

Design your own pushcart.

- Use the computer to design and draw your pushcart.
- Use Kids Pix Studio Deluxe. Select 'Paint a picture' and use the tools to draw a bird's eye view of your design.

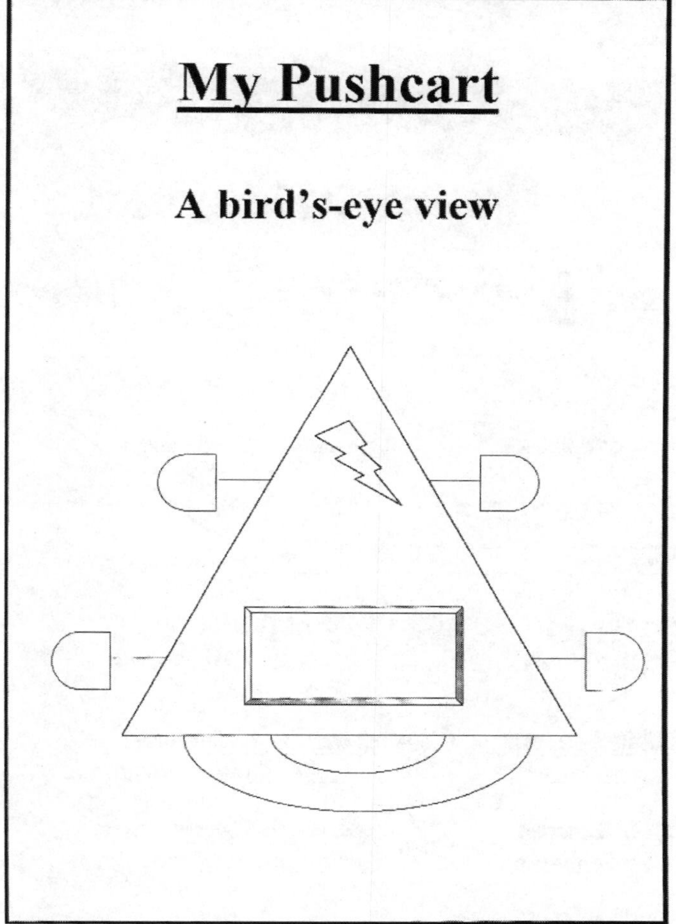

ICT skills

File management
Graphics

Software

Kid Pix Studio Deluxe

Snowboarding Diary

Snowboarding research

Find out more information about snowboarding.

- Using a computer with access to the Internet, find the Yahooligans search engine at **http://www.yahooligans.com**
- Key in 'snowboarding' and click on 'search' to view some sites.
- Prepare a list of ten things you have learnt about snowboarding.

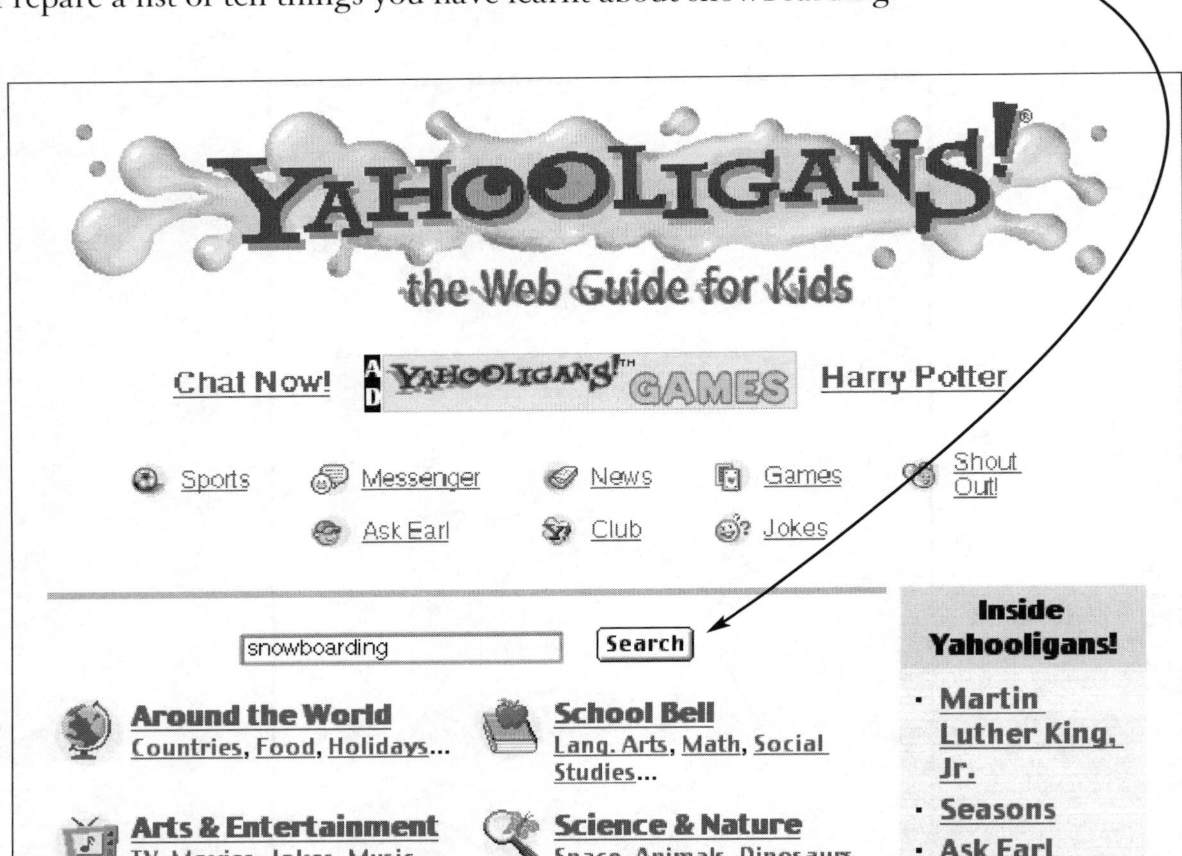

ICT skills

File management
Word processing
Electronic
Communication

Software

Netscape
Internet Explorer

Skateboarding

Skateboarding Research

Find out more information about skateboarding.

- Using a computer with access to the Internet, find the Yahooligans search engine at **http://www.yahooligans.com**
- Key in 'skateboarding' and click on 'search' to select five sites that could help Todd learn all about skateboarding.

Follow the steps to design your own skateboard, using the Internet.

- Using a computer with Internet access, go to **http://www.ccs.com**
- Enter the 'Skate store' and go to 'How to assemble skateboards.' Follow the steps to design your board.
- Share your ideas with your friends.

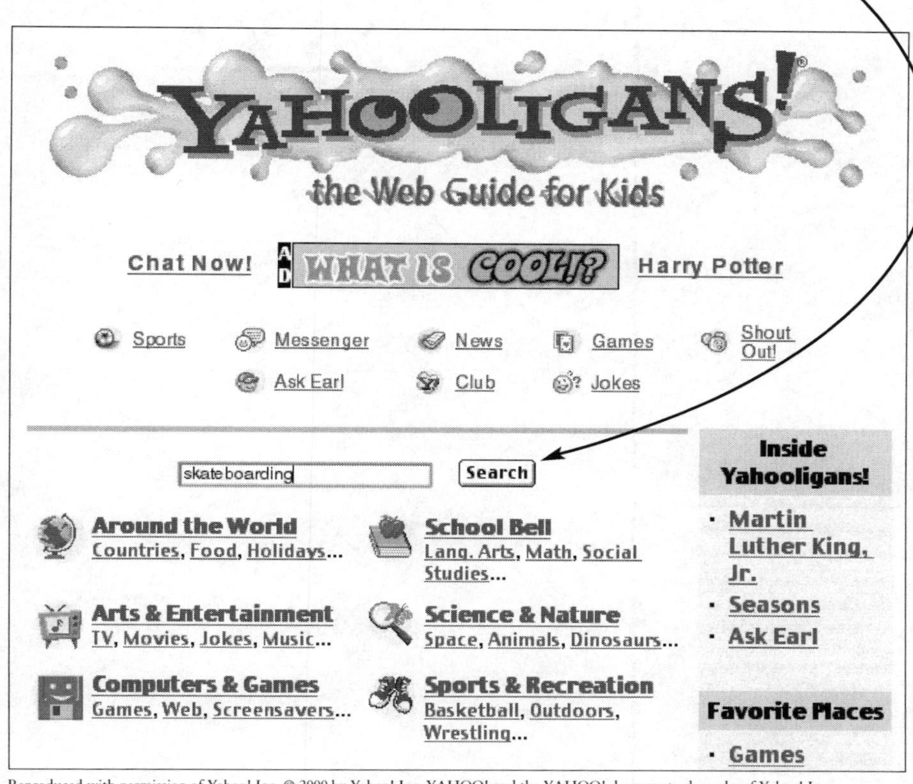

ICT skills

File management
Word processing
Electronic
Communication

Software

Netscape
Internet Explorer

Kites

Design and draw

Design your own kite.

- Use the computer to design and draw your kite.
- Using Microsoft Office or another application, use the drawing tools to create your design.

ICT skills

File management
Graphics

Software

Microsoft Office
Appleworks
Kid Pix Studio Deluxe

The Bicycle Book

Make a list of safety and maintenance tips

The Bicycle Book gives you lots of tips about bike riding and caring for your bike.

- Use a word processing program to prepare a list of things you have learnt about bicycles.
- Print out your information.
- With a friend, compare the things you have both learnt about bicycles.

ICT skills

File management
Word processing

Software

Microsoft Office
Appleworks

Funny Business: An Anthology of Humour

Design a poster

Design a poster to advertise *Funny Business: An Anthology of Humour*.

- Use a software program like Kid Pix Studio Deluxe or Microsoft Word to design your poster, using text and graphics.
- The poster should encourage other students to read the book. It should include:
  - a catchy headline. (Include action phrases like Watch Out! Grab It Now!, etc.)
  - the title and the author of the book.
  - three main features of the book
  - the best things about the book.

  where to buy a copy!

RUTLAND ELEMENTARY SCHOOL

ICT skills

File management
Word processing
Graphics

Software

Kid Pix Studio Deluxe
Microsoft Word